HIDDEN THORNS

Knights of the Gleam

L. B. ANNE

JOA PRESS

Florida

For information, Address JOA Press

P.O. Box 7984, Seminole, Florida 33775.

www.joapress.com

Cover art © 2023 by BRoseDesignz

Edited by Cristy Watson

Unless otherwise indicated, scripture quotations are from the New King James Version Copyright ©1982 by Thomas Nelson, Inc. Used by permission.

Library of Congress Control Number: 2024909995

ISBN 979-8-9889776-1-2

HIDDEN & THORNS

Knights of the Gleam

Other books by L. B. Anne:

The Sheena Meyer Series:
The Girl Who Looked Beyond the Stars
The Girl Who Spoke to the Wind
The Girl Who Captured the Sun
The Girl Who Became a Warrior
City of Gleamers
Secret of Shadow and Light
May Your Vision Be True
Fate of the Gleam Keeper

Knights of the Gleam Series:
Angel Girl Awakening
Hidden Thorns

Everfall Series:
Before I Let Go
If I fail
All the Scars

For Diana

"Out of suffering have emerged the strongest souls; the most massive characters are seared with scars."

Kahlil Gibran

CHAPTER 1

SHEENA

The thing about sadness...it sucks! It can overtake you to the point where you rule out all the things you know to be true and reasonable. But when sadness evolves into rage...there is no limit to the destruction it can bring. It can take on a life of its own, a destructive force that levels even the strongest of wills. That's what I worried would happen to my friends.

Even as I was being absorbed into the Murk, almost becoming one with it, at least for a moment, I managed to hold onto myself and my own thoughts. I clung to them desperately as the Murk attacked my mind, trying to send everything that made me *me*, into oblivion.

A strange cloudiness surrounded my mind and body. Its force tightened around me, and I was certain its strengthening was coming from my friends—whatever they were feeling because of what happened to me.

Anger is not the answer. I willed the thought to the Knights, hoping it would reach them. Hoping it would help them. Not that I had ever been able to send them a thought before, but now, because of the awakening...maybe. What they did in the next few hours would determine my fate. Somehow I knew that and that they needed Phoenix—all the Knights.

Anger will only lead you down a path of destruction and fuel the Murk. Control it and find Phoenix. Chana, I know you can hear me. Tell them!

The Murk pulled me away in a suffocating grip. Its fury and malevolence crushing the breath of hope within me.

"The devil you know is better than the devil you don't," Nana once told me. We didn't know anything about this devil. It was time we did. I stopped fighting and allowed my body to relax. The Murk held me in an inescapable grip. Smog permeated every inch of my being, and each inhale was like breathing in hot embers. My lungs were being smothered by the ever-thickening haze, and my coughs echoed around me.

With my last breath, I opened my eyes, barely making out the hands reaching for me. My arms were like heavy weights as I grabbed one of the hands. The heat from the grasp burned against my skin and I winced, gritting my teeth as I held on tightly, determined not to let go. *It's freeing Draven!*

Suddenly, the hand violently tore away. Panic and desperation coursed through me as I frantically reached out, searching for him. My mind raced. The only solution was clear, but the weight of its implications made me hesitate. How could I do this to my family? What if it killed me? But then again, who else would face the Murk for the sake of Draven? A sense of duty and selflessness overtook me, as the swirling smog filled my lungs. "Draven, I will take your place," I managed. "Let him go now."

A booming voice echoed in my mind. "You would sacrifice yourself for him? Foolish girl," the creature jeered.

I could still hear my father screaming for me to free myself, but it was too late. I had already made my decision. I could no longer see anyone. All I had to go on was my faith as I was held in a lion's den, waiting to be devoured.

I closed my eyes and focused on my family and my friends, knowing that this was the right thing to do. The Murk's molten intensity stopped pulsing around me. Light shone through my lids, as if the sun had just come out, shining brightly after a vicious storm, and I opened my eyes.

The Murk was gone. I surveyed everything around me, my eyes wide with surprise, as I breathed in fresh air. I was in a palace with marble statues, gold chandeliers, and the most beautiful garden I had ever seen.

"Sheena, I'm here," Draven's weak voice called.

"Where are you?" I spun around, but I couldn't see him. "Is this what you do to them?" I yelled at the Murk. "You keep them blinded by illusions? Draven," I called. For all I knew, he was right beside me. "You said if I surrendered to you, you would let him go."

"I lied."

CHAPTER 2

THEODORE

The smell of burning insulation filled the air, taking me back to that one time lightning struck near my house. The lingering scent of sulfur and smoke added to the heavy atmosphere. In the dim light, our breaths formed small clouds in the cold air, their wisps dancing momentarily before dissipating into the eerie night.

I had watched in shock as the Murk engulfed Sheena, churning around her until she disappeared. She didn't even scream. The Knights of the Gleam stood frozen in disbelief, as the Murk lifted higher in the sky. Time seemed to stand still, as if the scene were a video and the world had pressed pause. We were stranded in misery.

"Sheena," I cried and frantically searched the sky for any sign of her. The Murk loomed overhead, dense and suffocating clouds of smoldering smoke, almost taunting us by concealing Sheena just beyond our grasp. My heart pounded so hard, I thought it might explode from my chest.

"Theodore, she's gone. What can we do?" Bradly's hands grabbed hold of me, but I pulled them away from my jacket. The last thing I wanted was to be touched. I couldn't bear the thought of being consoled or participating in a collective display of grief and pity with her or anyone else. Not yet.

She went to Logan next. "What are we going to do now? Logan, tell us!" She looked away from him as he stared ahead with his mouth open, unable to respond.

Bradly's panting breaths quickened as she shifted her attention to Corey. Her voice trembled. "Can't you do something?"

But none of us were responsive, and Bradly collapsed to her knees, tears streaming down her face.

Although our group fell silent, it was me who kept yelling Sheena's name. But it didn't matter how much I screamed, the Murk's whirring tornado of a force soon drowned me out. We waited in angst, thinking Sheena was going to come bursting out of it, turning the Murk to ashes. But minutes passed and she did not.

Logan finally snapped out of his daze, looked over his shoulder, and locked eyes with me. "Theodore, stop screaming. Listen to me. We can't give up," he said. "We can't just stand here."

"But what can we do? We don't know where she is or how to get to her," said Cameron, his voice anxious.

"Logan is right," I told them. We couldn't just stand there and mourn. We had to take action.

"Okay," Bradly sniffed and stood, pulling herself together. She wiped away her tears with the back of her hand and pushed her long braids inside the collar of her coat. "Let's do it then."

"It's on you," Logan told Corey.

On Corey?

Corey nodded. "Let's use what we have. Together."

"What are we about to do?" I asked Logan as Corey turned to where the Murk loomed in the air. "*You're* the leader," I told him.

"Yeah, but I'm not supposed to be."

"Knights!" Corey shouted. He lifted his arms and charged forward. We followed suit, our feet pounding over the snow-covered ground. A blue neon light shone through Corey's sleeves, as his arms lit up with angelic symbols.

My hands tingled. The same glow flowed through to my fingertips.

"Now!" Corey exclaimed. We watched him and repeated his motion, slamming our forearms together and thrusting our fists toward the ground. The gleam flickered beneath our skin—the full force of what that angel had given us. All at once, we unleashed a wave of energy that cracked the pavement and rippled up into the air, slashing through the Murk's smoke screen.

The Murk roared, a defiant cry against our collective forces. And in a desperate attempt to cripple it, Seren's arms shot in front of her and a force somehow connected to Ariel and Mr. Meyer, intertwining through them in an intricate dance. Their bodies became a blur of swirling energy. The air crackled with electricity as they formed a single, focused burst of power. The ground trembled beneath us as the intensity increased, causing the Murk to roar and recoil.

As it lowered toward the ground, the Murk's smoky form wavered and flickered, weakened by the onslaught of our collective might.

"It's working!" yelled Parker.

For a brief moment, I had hope that we could retrieve Sheena and finally kill this thing. *Come on, Sheena. Get out of there.*

"Oh no. What's it doing?" yelled Cameron.

A dark figure stepped forward out of the Murk. He raised his hand, and tendrils of black burning lava shot out towards Ariel, Seren, and Mr. Meyer. A gust of wind suddenly whipped through the air, carrying with it a faint whisper. Dingy sped by, somehow grabbing the three of them out of its grasp.

"That was fun," said Drake, as he backed inside the Murk and disappeared.

"No!" I yelled. "Sheena!"

The Murk lifted, as if to say: *My work is done here. Off I go, see ya.*

We all screamed and ran toward it.

I thought I was going to lose my mind. I pounded my chest. "Me, take me! I'm right here! Take me!"

"Theodore! Stop!" Chana shouted, coming out of nowhere and grasping my shoulders. The white fur-lined hood of her coat slid back from her face, revealing a pained expression that mirrored my own agony. I pulled away. Tears fell from my cheek onto my lip, salty and warm. I wanted to feel all the anger and regret that usually comes within moments after making a bad decision. I should have demanded Sheena stay home—duct taped her to the chair in her basement. Anything, so that she wasn't with us at the trailer park, facing off against the Murk, and then being taken by it.

"What is happening here?" yelled Quincy. "I don't understand. We were supposed to win this. Weren't we?" She turned away from us. "I save you, God saves me," she said over and over and charged after the Murk. Justin ran after her and caught her around the waist, pulling her back as she tried to fight him.

"Stop. What are you doing?" he yelled.

I had no idea where Quincy was trying to run to. The Murk was already gone. The night air was now crisp with no sign of smoke. Still, it was almost impossible to breathe.

I grabbed my head. *I've always protected her, even when we were kids. When she tried to befriend a dog that wanted to eat her alive, I was there, pushing her behind me and holding a stick at it until her mother found us. When she was being bullied or the subject of day's gossip at school for dressing in a crazy combination of colors and patterns, I defended her. But I couldn't this time.*

"What did we do?" asked Jasmine. "We shouldn't have come here."

"Failed her, is what we did," said Bodhi.

We were all silent for a moment, absorbed in our own thoughts as the wind blew and it was suddenly much colder than it had been when we arrived.

I watched Chana closely for signs she might break down. She only stared at the ground as sirens blared in the distance. Her hair, twisted into tight ringlets that hung from under her white hat, danced wildly in the wind. Suddenly, she met my gaze, peering through her tousled locks.

"I...I hear her."

Heads lifted and everyone turned to Chana. Mr. Meyer approached her. We surrounded the two of them.

"You hear her?" he asked. "How do you hear her?"

"I don't know," she said. "Wait." Her hand flew up to keep anyone from saying another word. She closed her eyes. "Find Phoenix."

"Find Phoenix?" I choked out. Someone might as well have punched me in the stomach. The realization that my best friend might be gone because of Phoenix was too much. My first thought was, as Corey used to say, *He's about to meet these fists.*

Chana looked around at us and then turned to Logan. "He's a Knight of the Gleam, isn't he? He's supposed to be here. Why didn't he come tonight?"

Logan frowned. "I don't know, but I'm sure as heck going to find out."

CHAPTER 3
LOGAN

I was not okay. The Murk had taken a knife and severed my soul tie to Sheena. That's what it felt like—a knife dug into us and cut us apart. She and I were connected as cousins and as gleamers. Now, I couldn't understand how I was so angry with her about my father. It was never her fault that he died. He forced my hand, and I chose to save her. But when she most needed me to come to her aid, I failed. After following her and keeping an eye on her when she was in middle school, to protect her from the Murk, I still let it take her. *How? Why?* I accepted the blame for all of it. Inside, I was torn to pieces and was now tearing those pieces to shreds. But I couldn't allow the others to see how broken I was.

"Logan, it's not a good idea to be here when the police arrive," said Uncle Jonas. Though his eyes were red, he maintained a composed demeanor. I couldn't fathom the emotions he must be experiencing after witnessing his daughter being taken.

"Huh? Oh, yes, I agree."

"But Michelle..." said Seren, referring to our classmate who had been held captive by Maria. One of Corey's Bodyguard co-workers knelt beside her.

Seren shot Maria a menacing look.

"She's safe with me now. I won't hurt her," Maria replied. She was shivering now too, being no longer infected by the Murk.

Ariel edged closer to Michelle. "I'll stay with her."

"No, you won't," I replied, not trying to boss her around, but there was no way I was letting her out of my sight.

"It's okay, Logan. I'll stay too," said Seren.

"Neither of you will. Let's go." I ushered both of them ahead of me.

Corey nodded toward his friends.

"We've got her," one of the boys said, indicating they would stick around to make sure Michelle was safe.

"Chana," said Corey.

She lifted her phone. "Already on it. My dad is on duty tonight. He's probably with the officers headed this way. Don't worry, he'll make sure your bodyguard boys don't have any problems."

"Good."

"Listen here, Maria," Seren snapped, over her shoulder. "You better tell the truth."

I doubted Maria or Michelle would even remember we were there. The kids we saved rarely did.

"Hurry," said Uncle Jonas.

We ran toward the trailer park entrance as a car skidded over the ice and pulled up in front of us.

"Nana?"

She opened the driver's side door and stepped out. "Come on! Hurry!"

By the look on her face, Nana knew everything that had happened. "We have twenty-four hours, at most. Sheena is strong. She can fight it. You raised her right—in the fear of the Lord," she told Uncle Jonas. "If it takes any longer than that, we may lose her."

"How do you know that?" I asked.

Nana's voice was strained. "Don't worry about how I know. We need to hurry."

"Do you know what it is doing to her in there?" asked Teila.

"No one knows."

"Yes, someone does," said Cameron.

"He's right," I replied. I understood where he was going. Just like how we needed to talk to Phoenix and Quincy because of their experiences with the Murk.

"Where are the twins?" Cameron asked.

I motioned to the two girls, barely conscious after being pulled out of the Murk by Sheena.

"Everyone to my house," Uncle Jonas yelled over us.

"Who's taking them?" asked Justin as he knelt and picked up one of the girls.

"This way," said Corey, carrying the other girl. "Put them in the backseat of my car."

Ariel's eyes met mine. "I need to ride with them."

"No, you don't," I responded firmly.

"Yes, I do. Being a healer gleamer is my priority, no matter what you're worried about."

The look she gave me held so much authority that I didn't even think about arguing with her. A twinge of shame settled in my gut for trying to protect her, but it was quickly overshadowed by the disappointment on her face as she turned away. I knew better; a gleamer's assignment always came first, regardless of our feelings.

"I'll ride with them," said Seren, giving me a reassuring look. And after what I had seen her do against the Murk, when she wasn't even a Knight of the Gleam, I felt better about Ariel riding in Corey's car with the twins. They sat on either side of the twins, who looked confused and barely aware of what was happening.

The four of us—Theodore, Chana, Dingy, and I—rode in the backseat of Nana's sedan. We were just as tense inside the car as we were outside of it. Nana drove, and Uncle Jonas sat in the front passenger seat.

Quincy drove her car. Parker, Bradly, and Teila rode with her. For the moment, Quincy and Bradly were getting along, united by their worry for Sheena.

Everyone else followed in Justin's truck.

I wasn't sure if it was safe for Nana to drive, because someone else always drove her around, like she couldn't see well or something. But she sped along the highway like she never needed our assistance in the first place. Maybe it was just the company she wanted. Or maybe it was all a farce, so the Murk would never know how strong she really was.

CHAPTER 4

THEODORE

Though we rode in a large sedan, we were squished together in the backseat. *Like sardines in a can*, I thought. Remembering the time that Sheena had a full-blown tantrum over sardines while we were kids made me smile internally, despite my mounting anxiety. Fish with heads missing and trapped in a can? She couldn't understand it. I had been around to witness most of her tantrums over the years. Scenes that only best friends were privy to. Me, Sheena, and Chana. Our trinity of friendship was now shattered, leaving me with the unbearable weight of reality pressing down on my chest. Where was God? Why did he let this happen? Where was Sheena's guardian angel? Was Sheena's destiny to be a martyr? I shook my head, searching for thoughts that could help us.

The street lights played across our faces in waves as I stared straight ahead at the armrest and cup holder between the front seats, unwilling to contemplate what we were speeding towards...

or what could be waiting for us when we got there. *This is a dream. It has to be. I'm dreaming. Wake Up!*

Suddenly, Dingy whispered, "No, it's not a dream." His voice was barely audible. I nodded absentmindedly. *Did I say that out loud?*

The scenery outside the window was a jumble of shapes and shadows. Trees, storefronts, and other structures all passed by in a blur. I was lost in thought for the rest of the ride, hardly paying attention when we finally arrived at Sheena's house.

We pulled into the driveway with the other vehicles behind us. Corey parked on the snowy lawn, while Quincy parked behind us, and Justin blocked the driveway by parking in front of the sidewalk.

Mr. Meyer hurried and unlocked the side door of the house. We all crowded inside the entry and spilled into the kitchen.

Justin and Corey carefully brought the twins indoors. The way they carried them reminded me of injured children being hefted into their home by their parents after falling off their bikes. They set the pair down in the hall outside of the kitchen and helped them stand, if you could call it standing. The two were hunched over like pill bugs about to curl up. They grabbed onto each other's arms as if they were afraid we were going to separate them. Their identical faces pressed together, both with blackened lips and cracked brown-gray complexions.

The only distinguishing marks between them were the cuts, bruises, ash, and burn marks that covered any exposed skin. A mix of odors—smoke, singed flesh, and burnt hair—permeated from them.

The twins looked up at us with fear in their eyes, fear that only a few of us understood. The Murk had infected me and Bradly before, so we knew how they felt. Quincy knew also, maybe more.

My mind may have been playing tricks on me, but there was a concern on Mr. Meyer's face, and Nana's, that I hadn't noticed before.

"We should've taken them to the hospital, not here," said Teila, watching the twins. "They need help."

"No," said Nana. "This is the safest place for them right now. And for any others."

"Others? Why?" asked Teila.

"If the Murk wants them back, it will tear a hospital apart to get to them."

No one argued or said anything further. I don't think it had occurred to any of us that the Murk might want the twins back. Nana was one of the oldest gleamers I knew—a descendant of the City of Gleamers. She probably gained this insight from experience. But we had witnessed it also, when the Murk blew up Mr. Tobias's house. The reporter on the news said it was a gas leak. We were there; we knew better. A chill ran up my spine as Chana squeezed in beside me.

Logan took a step towards the girls, but they cowered away from him before he could extend a hand. His face fell with realization. "Right...it's too soon...no sudden movements."

Dingy had been so quiet that I forgot he was there until he placed his hand in mine. I realized he should be in bed, but I was apprehensive about approaching Mr. Meyer about it. His shoulders were raised up to his ears, and his jaws clenched, as though at any moment, he would bend a steel beam in half. "Do... Do you want me to take Dingy home?" I asked.

"No. Not yet," he replied, not even looking in my direction. "He's been revealed as a gleamer. He stays with us."

The warrior child I had witnessed at the trailer park now looked so sad. He squeezed my hand, and wouldn't let go.

Parker scratched his beard. "Speaking of Dingy, I know we're all distraught right now and everything, but are we going to ignore the fact that this kid came flying through the air?"

"Parker..."

"What? No one has said anything about it. That was the craziest—"

"What are you, five? How was that the craziest? We are—how many of us are there? Thirteen? Maybe twelve—give or take—kids fighting with the help of angels against a giant glob of lava and smoke shooting tentacles at us, and one that sucked up our friend," said Justin. He pushed past Parker. "Nothing we see is crazy anymore."

"I didn't save her," Dingy cried.

The others moved away as Chana knelt beside him. "I need you to be strong...For Sheena. Can you do that?"

Dingy wiped his eyes with the back of his hand and nodded.

"You did the best you could. Better than any of us. And you helped save all of our lives. Don't worry, we'll get her back."

I shook my head at Chana. *Don't lie to him.* She had said too much. I wanted to believe it too, but she shouldn't have told him that.

"Promise?" asked Dingy.

Don't do it, Chana.

"Absolutely, Dingleberry."

And now you're promising? Really?

Dingy sniffed. "You always call me weird stuff."

"Right you are, Dingy Booty."

I think I saw a hint of a smile from that one.

All of our team were either leaning against the wall staring at the floor, grabbing water, pacing, or sitting and staring into space, looking defeated, when feet bounded the stairs. Rapid, impatient steps neared us. Some of us stepped back.

Her colorful headscarf caught my attention first, followed by the robe that she had tightly cinched around her waist. Her face was creased with confusion and worry. "Uh, hello...I think?" She looked past us at Mr. Meyer. "Jonas, what—"

"Belinda, these girls need to be cleaned up and clothed quickly. We need to talk to them."

One twin grabbed the arm of the other, once again, afraid we were going to separate them.

"Oh my goodness. What happened to you?" she asked, reaching toward one of the girls.

Nana looked into the hall from the kitchen. "I'll make soup," she said, giving Mr. Meyer a curious look.

He shook his head. "No. There's no time."

"They're weak," said Nana.

Mr. Meyer squinted and squeezed the bridge of his nose. "Give them that soup-in-a-bowl stuff that Sheena likes to eat after school…" his voice trailed off.

"That's not what it's called," whispered Parker.

"Some of my pot liquor is what they need," said Nana.

Jasmine wrinkled her nose. "What's that?"

"The broth from the greens she cooks," said Logan.

Mrs. Meyer craned her neck to see around us. Her eyes met mine and seized my soul. "Theodore…" she began.

I looked away. I couldn't be the one to tell her.

"But where is—"

Everyone was silent. Nana had even stopped the running water that flowed into the teakettle. The only sound was the ticking of the clock on the wall in the foyer that reminded me of a countdown—to what I didn't know.

Someone tell her, I thought.

"Bee, this is urgent," said Mr. Meyer.

She moved slowly at first, still looking into her husband's eyes. She spoke softly and calmly, like she would have if she had found two hurt kittens in an alleyway, instead of these girls with half-healed wounds that nobody knew how they had acquired. Then she led Chana, Ariel, Seren, and Teila taking the twins upstairs. Quincy, Bradly, and Jasmine stayed behind with us.

"What is this soot all over them?" Mrs. Meyer asked, as they climbed the steps.

"We don't know," Chana responded. She looked back at me with wide eyes and shrugged.

'Don't tell her,' I mouthed.

Chana nodded.

"What now?" asked Logan after they were out of sight.

Without a word, Mr. Meyer took off up the stairs. Logan glanced at me and followed him.

TIME REMAINING: 23 HOURS

CHAPTER 5

BRADLY

I waited for something to happen, but I didn't know what. Sitting and being still was not an option of me. We needed to be doing something. It was legit, nerve-wracking.

To get away from everything for a moment, I went into the half bath under the stairs, and turned on the faucet. My fingers were covered in whatever was all over the twins, black and smudged, like I'd been playing in the cooled charred embers of a fire. The warmth of the water calmed my trembling hands, and I stared at the flow washing over them, as if it would reveal how to get Sheena back. How could I save my friend-turned-enemy-turned-friend again? That's who we had been to each other from kindergarten until now.

I sighed heavily. The rift in our relationship wasn't exactly Sheena's fault. I had changed and Sheena hadn't, and not just our bodies, as Sheena liked to point out. I morphed into a woman earlier than she did. As a result, we no longer cared about the same things. For me, it was boys and makeup, and becoming an influencer. But for Sheena, her focus never changed. It remained on friends, family, and saving the earth.

Yeah, Sheena always wanted to save things, even us. But look what good that did her.

I bit my lip as I watched the water puddle in my hands. These thoughts were useless right now. Still, I ached inside, wondering, *why her?* Why was she the one the angels chose? Why did she have to die? Why couldn't I be as cold as I used to be, so this wouldn't hurt so much? I rubbed my hands together so hard that they ached, as if trying to scrub away all that had happened that morning. The Murk, Maria, the twins, Sheena—it was all in my head and on my hands, and I wanted to erase it all. I envied the kids who knew nothing of the Murk or the evil that existed in the world.

I fought back the urge to cry, held on to the sink, and took a deep breath.

Someone tapped on the door. "Hey, are you okay in there?"

For the first time, I looked at the mirror, ignored the girl I saw there, and instead saw the same thing I kept playing over and over in my head: the Murk taking Sheena.

Don't, I told myself, but the tears came anyway. I didn't realize I had made a sound, but my mouth was open. A line of snot connected from my top lip to my lower.

"I'm coming in," she said.

I pulled my braids to one side and splashed water onto my face before she could see me. The door opened.

Quincy immediately scanned my face, searching for unspoken answers that lay in my tear-filled gaze. "Are you okay?" she asked again.

We both looked up, hearing feet running up the stairs.

"I don't think that's a fair question," I replied as I took a hand towel from a hook on the wall and rubbed it over my face. "None of us are okay."

"Look at you. You're smearing eyeliner across your cheek."

I glanced in the mirror. "Oh crap. I forgot."

"Stay here, I've got you," said Quincy. She hurried out of the bathroom and came back with a bottle of olive oil.

"What am I supposed to do with that?"

"Soap is harsh. It can ruin the pH of your skin. Use a little of this and you can wipe the eyeliner right off." She removed the cap and turned the bottle over on some tissue she had wadded up, set the bottle on the sink, and dabbed the tissue on my face, wiping away the black smudges. I watched as she worked, her touch gentle, but sure.

As she finished, I smirked. "Why are you being nice to me?"

She tossed the tissue in the trash can beside the sink. "Maybe because we're on the same team. And we care about the same girl. And I'm not a heartless monster."

I nodded.

"And you're not being annoying right now," she added.

I smiled at her, and she nudged me with her shoulder.

As we stood there, I couldn't help but notice the way her hazel eyes sparkled in the dim light of the bathroom. Quincy had always been a mystery to me, and such a hothead. But for the moment, I was glad she was there.

We both jumped, hearing a knock on the door. "Corey wants to talk to everyone. Now," said Jasmine. We exchanged a look before rushing out of the bathroom, down the hall, and into the family room.

Corey was already seated, looking impatient as we entered. "Yo, where the heck have you been?" he demanded.

He gestured for us to sit and we took our respective seats—Quincy beside me on the couch. "We were in the bathroom," I replied.

Corey's eyes flicked to Quincy. "And where were you?" he asked, as if he didn't believe what I had just said. Actually, I hardly believed we were getting along.

"I was helping her clean up," Quincy said calmly.

Corey lifted a brow and moved on from us.

"All right, listen up," he began. "This whole thing is a real mess, but we can't let it weaken us. Fear and worry will only work against us. We have a job to do, and we need to stay focused."

I nodded along with the rest of the group, but Quincy shook her head and moved to the edge of her seat.

"Corey, if we are going to talk about anything, talk specifically about saving Sheena. That's it. That's all I want to hear. Less than twenty-four hours, her grandmother said? What are we going to do about that, Chief?"

"Don't call me 'Chief,'" said Corey, "And you're not wrong, but if you don't all calm down and remember who we are—not you, Quincy—"

"Because you're not a Knight," I whispered.

"—any plan we come up with is going to fail," said Corey. "We're exhausted, hungry, and hurting. That's a messed up combination to work from." He glanced at Quincy. "So like I was saying...mindset is everything. Take a beat and get yourself together. We will regroup in fifteen with faith, rather than fear. I'm serious. Don't come back here with an all-is-lost attitude. You have fifteen minutes to release every tear." He stood and clapped once. "Let's get to it."

Quincy opened her mouth to argue, but I put a hand on her arm to stop her. Her brows rose, and I silently shook my head. We couldn't afford to argue right now.

"Okay, Corey," she replied.

CHAPTER 6
THEODORE

I climbed the stairs after Mr. Meyer and Logan, tugging Dingy along with me. Bodhi followed also. I glanced over the banister at the Knights who were in the hall. Corey gestured for them to stay back.

Mr. Meyer stormed into Sheena's bedroom. It was neat, for Sheena. I wondered if she knew someone would be in her bedroom without her, snooping around. Mr. Meyer tore the room apart, throwing open the dresser drawers. Clothes flew through the air. Next, he tossed items from her shelves: photos, books, and figurines with giant bobbleheads.

"Boys, search over there," he said, pointing hastily at the closet.

"What are we looking for?" I asked.

"Those books Sheena was reading by Stephen Woodruff. Journals. Notepads. There has to be something here. Sheena always knew more about what was happening than she let on. I am certain this time is no different."

We flipped over Sheena's mattress and scanned every book left on her shelves while Bodhi attempted to hack into her laptop.

I stared down at the Sailor Moon T-shirt we tossed down from the top shelf of the closet. It landed near Dingy's feet. Sheena hadn't worn it since the last time we went to the Comic-Con. I picked it up and ran my fingers over the familiar fabric, feeling a wave of nostalgia wash over me.

My eyes watered.

"Stop it. Don't do that," whispered Logan.

I nodded and quickly dried my eyes, hearing Bodhi ask a question.

"I can't get in. What's the password?

Mr. Meyer tucked in his lips and rubbed his goatee. "Any ideas, boys?"

"Something she was crazy about. Try Stevie Nicks," said Logan.

Bodhi typed quickly. "It didn't work."

"Try Fleetwood Mac."

"Nope."

"No, that's too easy." I thought for a moment.

Dingy pulled at my arm. "*Landslide.*"

My eyes widened. Dingy always knew things. That was one of Sheena's favorite songs. "Try Stevie Nicks–no, Fleetwood Mac 19... Umm... 19..."

"1975," said Mr. Meyer.

Bodhi tapped the keyboard. "That's it, I'm in."

"Look for any correspondence or anything related to the Murk or gleamers," said Mr. Meyer. "Check her history."

Bodhi tapped over the keyboard. "Uh... Sheena was researching guardian angels."

"That's not surprising," I replied. "Since she could see angels sometimes."

"Wait a minute," said Logan. He ran from the room and came back. "Here," he said, handing Mr. Meyer a journal.

"What's this?"

"It belonged to Drake. It's a journal he kept."

My head snapped toward him, realizing what it was. I replayed the whole scene of Sheena discovering an envelope with her name written on it at Draven's house. *She took it from that hidden room after I told her not to? I should have known. So that's what was inside.*

"Where did you get this?"

"It's a long story," said Logan. "Sheena was reading it."

Mr. Meyer opened the book and flipped through a few pages, stopping in the middle section. Before he could go any further, someone rushed through the hallway, feet bounded down the stairs, and then Sheena's mother shouted.

Mr. Meyer slammed the book shut and hurried from the bedroom. We went after him, except for Bodhi, who kept typing on the computer.

"Where is my child?" Sheena's mother cried.

"Belinda..." Nana said calmly.

"Don't 'Belinda' me. Where is my child?" Her voice was shrill and her eyes overflowed with tears. She turned to Mr. Meyer as he entered the room. "Don't lie to me, Jonas. Where is Sheena? You told me she would be safe." She looked around at us, wringing her hands, waiting for someone to answer. "What's happened to her? Why won't any of you tell me? Why isn't she here with you? Someone answer me!"

"What happened upstairs?" I whispered to Chana.

"She started asking questions, and we wouldn't answer her. She flipped out."

Mrs. Meyer turned to the girls. "Chana, Ariel..." Her eyes pleaded with them.

"The Murk—" Mr. Meyer started.

Mrs. Meyer slowly moved toward him. Her palm pressed against the wall as if guiding her on an escalator. Mr. Meyer opened his mouth, but nothing came out.

Nana moved closer to her and spoke up in a soft voice: "Belinda, dear...she's gone. The Murk has taken her."

Her face paled. She gasped and fell to her knees. "Nooooo!" she screamed, sobbing uncontrollably. Chana rushed forward and dropped beside her on the floor. She put her arms around Mrs. Meyer and rocked her gently, whispering words of comfort.

"She was so brave...she never stopped fighting for us—for what was right," Ariel said quietly, wiping a tear away from her eye. I saw Quincy swallow hard. Bradly shook her head at Ariel to not to say anything further. She was right, it wasn't helping.

I didn't know about anyone else, but Mrs. Meyer's cries made me shiver. She expressed exactly what I was feeling—what we were all probably feeling. Her fists clenched against the sides of her head as Mr. Meyer lifted her away, but she wouldn't stop screaming.

Nana followed them.

My back slid against the wall as I sank to the floor.

"Can we give her a sedative?" Parker asked.

"This is not a movie. People don't just have sedatives lying around in their homes," said Justin.

"Everybody..." was all Corey said and walked away.

Justin extended a hand to me, which I grasped, and pulled me up from the floor. We followed Corey into the kitchen and gathered around the island.

"Look, according to Nana, we have less than 24 hours left."

"Is it possible she could be wrong? How does she know that?" asked Teila.

"Who cares how she knows? I'm not taking any chances." He looked at his watch. "Actually, we are down to 22 hours. And we're wasting time."

"But the Murk—"

"This isn't about ridding the world of the Murk right now. Our only goal is to get Sheena out of that thing. Chana said she heard Sheena say, 'Find Phoenix', and I believe her," Corey turned to Logan. "Call him."

"It's almost 6 a.m. I doubt he'll answer, if he's even awake."

"Must be nice to be at home sleeping in your comfy bed while we're dealing with all of this," said Parker.

"If he doesn't answer, we're going to his house," said Chana. "I know what I heard. There must be a reason Sheena wants us to find him."

"You're not a Knight. How did you hear her when we didn't?" I asked. There was a part of me that felt if anyone was going to hear Sheena, it would have been me.

"Because all of you were too busy panicking."

"All the more reason why everybody needs to calm the heck down," said Corey.

Logan tapped on his cell phone.

"Put it on speaker," said Cameron. He had shared few words until now and mostly paced the floor.

The call connected after the third ring. I thought Phoenix's voicemail message would start, but there was only dead air. Logan looked at the phone, making sure it was still connected. "Hello?" he said. "Phoenix?"

"You soulless, rotten—I'm going to beat your—" Corey covered Cameron's mouth and Justin grabbed Cameron by the arms as he tried to yell, steering him away from Logan and pushing him to the family room.

"Ask him why—" I started.

Logan put a finger up and nodded, as if he knew what I was going to say. "What happened to you?" he asked Phoenix.

Still, there was nothing but silence.

"I'm good. I'm good," Cameron told Corey as he held his hands up. "Just leave me by myself a moment."

Corey and Justin let go of him and walked back over to the kitchen island.

"Phoenix?" Logan said again and looked up at us.

"Is he there?" asked Jasmine.

"He's there all right. He's listening, I bet," said Quincy. "Coward."

Logan's eyes narrowed, and he glanced at us one by one. "Phoenix, we know you can hear us. We—I need to know why you didn't show up. I know you have information that could help us. Are you there?"

Phoenix's voice finally broke through the silence. "I'm here, I'm here. I just... I-I need a moment," he stammered, his voice cracking.

The group exchanged frustrated looks. This wasn't the response we had hoped for.

Twenty-two hours. We didn't have time for the silent treatment. If Phoenix was stalling or refusing to speak, then he was going to hear what I had to say. "It took Sheena!" I exclaimed. "Do you hear me? The Murk took Sheena! And I don't know how, or why, but I think it's your fault. What did you do? Did you betray us?"

An agonizingly slow breath came from the other end of the line before Phoenix's broken voice finally spoke.

"It's true."

CHAPTER 7
THEODORE

There was another pause, this one longer than the last. When Phoenix finally spoke, his tone was different, more distant, as if he was holding something back. "I'm so sorry," he whispered. "Hold on. I'll be right back. I promise." He sounded like he was about to break down.

Seconds passed. "I'm back."

I spoke before Logan could. "What exactly is it that you're saying is true?" I needed to hear him say it, and I wanted the whole story, no matter how long it took.

Tires squealed outside. We turned toward the sound. Behind us, the family room was empty. Cameron was gone, and the back door of the house was wide open.

Corey patted the pockets of his coat and ran over to the kitchen window. "Yo, he took my car!"

Several of us went to the window also, as if we had to see his car missing for ourselves in order to believe it. Corey was right. His car was gone from the lawn, leaving tire tracks through the snow leading to the street. We hadn't even heard the alarm chirp when he opened the door.

"Where's Quincy?" asked Parker, looking around.

I searched for her sandy-brown afro puffs.

"She went too. I saw them go out the back door," said Bradly.

Corey turned to her, his face reddening. "And you didn't say anything?"

"I thought maybe Cameron wanted to cool off and needed air and that Quincy followed him out to help him calm down. You know they're cool. How was I supposed to know he would take your car keys and leave?"

"Crazy Quincy and angry Cameron? That's a bad mix," said Parker.

As they voiced their concerns, I watched Logan. He took his phone off speaker and held it to his ear. At the same time, Nana walked in, turned on the flame under the tea kettle and grabbed bottles of water from the counter. "The girls want to talk to you."

"Who? All of us?" I asked.

Corey shook his head as he returned from shutting the back door. "We don't have time for this. I mean, granted, they have information that can help us, but we need to split up. As I was about to suggest, one group can go up and talk to the twins. Another group needs to find out exactly what happened to Michelle. A group needs to look for clues. And a few of us need to go after Cameron before he does something dumb."

"I'm not saying you're wrong, and I admire your tenacity, but—" My attention switched to Logan, as he pocketed his phone. "Did you have a good private conversation?" I asked.

Logan frowned. "What's that supposed to mean?"

"What private conversation?" asked Corey.

I pointed at Logan. "It means you're hiding something."

"I'm not."

"Whose corner are you in?"

"What are you talking about?"

"Whose side are you on? You know exactly what I'm saying."

Logan shook his head. "You need to calm down, Theodore, because right now you sound just like Cameron."

"Maybe I should. Why didn't you keep the call on speaker, where we could all hear him? We know how much you cared about Phoenix and how much it messed you up discovering he wasn't really your brother. It sucked that it was a masquerade—a game you had been part of since you were a kid—to get close to you because of the Tobias bloodline. You didn't know the truth then, but now you do. He is not your brother, but Sheena *is* your blood."

"All type one gleamers are of the same bloodline," said Chana.

"Whatever. He knows what I mean. So who are you loyal to? Him, or Sheena?"

"Theodore..." Nana said gently, watching us. Everyone else neared cautiously.

"That's a stupid question," Logan replied and pushed past me. "Who's going up upstairs and who's going with me to Phoenix's?"

"I grabbed him. No, it isn't stupid. How do I know you and Phoenix aren't in cahoots?"

"Cahoots?" repeated Parker. "Who says that?"

I continued. "I'm telling you, don't let him go to Phoenix, Knights."

Logan turned back with a scowl. "As if you could stop me."

"Oh! Oh!" I said louder the second time. "Is that a threat? The way I see it, you killed your father to save Sheena's life..."

The energy in the room shifted as if everything had iced over. I'm sure everyone was contemplating what I said.

"You didn't want to do it right? I didn't consider it before, but now I figure you've always held a grudge against her."

"Have you?" asked Ariel.

Logan kept glancing over at her. "No, of course not. I mean, not like you think."

I stepped into his face. "So you did. Is this your revenge? Are you in on this with Phoenix?"

Ariel covered her mouth with both hands.

Dingy tugged at my arm, but someone guided him away.

"Are you forgetting I was right there with you, fighting alongside you to save her?" asked Logan.

I stepped so close to his face, I could feel his breath.

"Theodore, I think you need to back up," said Logan.

Corey extended an arm between us. "You guys need to stop."

We were eye to eye. "Or what? You're going to betray me like you did Sheena?"

Logan's fist came at me out of nowhere, too fast for me to even think about dodging it. Pain shot across my mouth and then my ear. I struck back, making contact with his jaw. The next thing I knew, Mr. Meyer was there, shoving me towards Corey with one hand, and pushing Logan away with the other.

It was a good thing Corey was holding me. I would have tried to charge through Sheena's father to get to Logan.

"What the heck is going on down here?" yelled Mr. Meyer.

Logan held his hand to the side of his face, and I held my ear. "You think just because you can shoot lightning from your hands that I'm afraid of you? At least you didn't get to warn Phoenix that Cameron is coming. I hope he bashes his head in," I muttered through a bloodied lip.

"That's enough, Theodore," Mr. Meyer exclaimed, still standing between us.

My eyes met Ariel's, and for a moment, I didn't like the person I saw in them. This wasn't me. But I knew if Sheena were here she would have helped me try to kick the crap out of him, too.

Mr. Meyer held Sheena's journal tightly in his hands and took a deep breath before speaking again. Annoyance filled his tone. "I'm trying to save my daughter. Do you understand? *My* daughter. The last thing we need right now is finger pointing and fighting against each other, dividing ourselves. What will it solve? Huh?" He looked back and forth at us.

I relaxed and stopped struggling against Corey. Logan saw that I relented, so he did as well. But then we both noticed that his phone had fallen from his pocket during the scuffle. It lay near Mr. Meyer's foot. We both dove for it. I snatched it from his grasp and tossed it to Chana before he could take it from me. If anyone had my back, she did. Without even thinking about it, she ran around the kitchen island.

"Hey!" yelled Logan.

Chana ran to the butler's pantry with Ariel following. Logan ran the other way, through the dining room to cut her off. Both entry doors closed with a soft thud, followed by the click of the locks engaging.

"Isn't someone going to do something?" asked Jasmine.

"They'll work it out. There are more important things to focus on. We're running out of time," said Mr. Meyer.

"That's exactly what I said," said Corey.

I stood outside of the butler's pantry, leaning against a cabinet. They weren't arguing in there, and Chana didn't sound like she was going to take that phone upside Logan's head if he didn't tell the truth. They were whispering.

A few minutes later, they exited the butler's pantry through the kitchen with Logan putting his phone in his front pocket. They all stopped in their tracks, surprised to see me standing there.

"So do you need to get your stories straight or what?" I asked.

"What are you talking about, Theodore?" asked Chana.

"You tell me. What did I just hear? You sure didn't threaten to chop him in the throat like you always do to me."

They exchanged glances, solidifying my assumptions. Something was up. What did the three of them know that I didn't?

"I have nothing to say to you," Logan responded, as he brushed past.

"Then why did you ask Chana about guarding Sheena? She isn't a Knight. And Ariel, you asked her if there is anything she can do? Why?"

Again, they glanced at each other.

"Stop doing that. Are you looking at each other for permission or something?"

"We need to find Phoenix. Sheena's life depends on it," said Chana. "That's all that's important right now."

I reluctantly followed them over to the others. Each sat on a different side of the room. Chana and I fussed a lot, but we were close—like brother and sister. I couldn't believe she was keeping something from me. She might as well have been choosing Logan over me. I shook my head to clear it. *Stop making it about you. Focus on Sheena,* I told myself.

"What's in the book, Mr. Meyer?" asked Jasmine.

"It belonged to Drake," he explained. "He left behind this journal, filled with his observations and insights about the Murk and the hidden thorns that lie within it."

"Hidden thorns?"

"Unseen dangers."

"Where did it come from?" asked Bradly.

"Logan?" said Mr. Meyer.

"I got it from Sheena. Well, she didn't exactly give it to me. It was on her nightstand..." His voice lowered and he rubbed his hand through his hair. "And I took it when she wasn't paying attention."

"Thief," I muttered.

"That's enough," said Mr. Meyer.

"So, what else is in there?" asked Jasmine.

All eyes turned towards Mr. Meyer, eager for more information.

"All right, I can see you're all curious. Let's make this quick." Mr. Meyer stood in the middle of the family room with us looking up at him from our seats.

Dingy clung to Chana now. His eyes slowly closing and him trying to fight against it, but losing the battle.

We were silent as Mr. Meyer turned the pages so carefully, I thought they might tear or catch fire if he moved too quickly. Finally, his eyes widened. "Listen to this," he said, his voice a mix of hope and concern. "Drake wrote: *Within the Murk lies the truth, but also the deception. It conceals hidden problems and difficulties, and the consequences of our actions are not always what they seem.*"

"What does that mean?" Ariel asked, her brows furrowed.

"It means that we can't trust what we see at face value," Logan replied. "The Murk distorts reality and creates illusions. We need to be cautious and look beyond the surface to find the truth."

"But how does that help us?" Seren asked. "Where do we even begin?"

Mr. Meyer flipped through a few more pages, reading aloud another passage from Drake's journal. "*The path to the Murk is hidden, but not impossible to find.* Then there's something here about electricity: *It holds the key to unlocking the secret to the hidden thorns.*"

"Electricity," Logan thought aloud, holding his chin.

Corey stood. "No disrespect, Mr. Meyer, but whoever wants to stay here and figure this out, go right ahead. Jasmine." Corey said firmly.

"I know, I know. Research. I'll get to work on it," she replied.

Corey turned to Mr. Meyer, and he nodded for him to continue. "Chana, you go up and see what the twins know. Call us with whatever you find."

Chana didn't move. Her focus was on the book Mr. Meyer held.

"What about you?" I asked Corey.

"I'm going after Cameron."

"To question Phoenix?"

"To bring him back here. We can't waste any more time. Whatever has to happen, I have a feeling he needs to be here."

"May I see it?" Chana asked, her voice barely above a whisper.

Mr. Meyer's forehead scrunched up like he was trying to solve a tough math problem.

"There might be answers or clues that I would understand because...because Sheena and I are best friends. It may give me an idea of what to ask the twins about."

Mr. Meyer nodded and handed the journal to her.

She thumbed through the pages and stopped. "So, this is interesting and weird that he wrote about this..."

Chana read aloud. Corey stopped walking and listened. "*If you throw something over a power line, it will go from phase to phase. Power has three phases: A, B, and C. This is the reason why you see three lines on a road going from pole to pole. The fourth line is neutral. If you throw a line over two of them, the wire will go phase to phase. Phase to phase is the action, and an explosion is the result.*

I know you're wondering what this has to do with anything. This is about energy. I just described the concept of electrical power transmission using three-phase power, which is a common method used in electric power systems.

Again, if you throw something, such as a wire, over two of these power lines, it will be in contact with two phases, or phase to phase. This is dangerous because the voltage between two phases is much higher than the voltage between one phase and the neutral line. If a wire comes into contact with two phases, it can cause a short circuit, which can cause an explosion, meaning serious damage.

Do you understand? I have outlined the potential dangers of coming into contact with multiple phases."

"Who is he talking to?" asked Justin.

I frowned. "I think to Sheena. But how? What does it mean?"

"Electricity," Logan said again. From the way his brows knit together, I could tell he was realizing something. He looked up, his eyes suddenly brighter. "I had a conversation with Sheena about electricity. I was working on a homework assignment on my laptop. She was messing with me, pointing at my screen, and saying my answer was incorrect. 'No, it isn't,' I told her. 'The flow of electrons between atoms is what we call electricity. Since our bodies are huge masses of atoms, we can generate elec—'" He stopped abruptly.

Mr. Meyer nodded as if he understood exactly what Logan was getting at.

"It's all connected, isn't it?" asked Seren.

TIME REMAINING: 20 HOURS

CHAPTER 8

SHEENA

A gust of wind rushed past me, catching every single raindrop as it fell from the sky and brushing them against the windows of the houses that lined my street. The stream that flowed from the downspouts transformed into a gentle trickle as the heavy downpour eased to a drizzle. In minutes, the sun broke through the clouds, casting a beautiful rainbow in the distant sky.

A small patch of vibrant green grass lined the path leading to my front porch. I had never been so happy to be home. I wanted to run at my house, the windows glistening in the sunlight; the warmest place in the world, up the front steps and inside to my parents. The safety of their embrace awaited me. When I found them, I planned to squeeze them tight and never let go.

Suddenly, the scene before me wavered and rippled like a mirage; the colors blurring and blending together in an unnatural way. The houses and streets that were once so clear and detailed now appeared distorted and almost surreal.

"It's an illusion," I whispered inside. I knew what it was doing. The Murk tried to show me what I loved—something good and peaceful, so I would stop fighting it. Darkness trying to masquerade as light.

A familiar voice called to me, its baritone reverberating through the air. He was beckoning.

I looked up, my heart racing as I saw him right there, right in front of me. He beamed like the sun as he smiled down at me.

"Sheena Meyer," Drake said. As always, he said my full name, making it seem like a curse.

"Aren't you going to say hello?" Drake asked, his voice dripping with honey. He chuckled, his eyes sparkling with amusement. "Oh, Sheena Meyer, you're still as skittish as ever." Not a hair was out of place. His skin was smooth and even-toned. He looked healthy. "Relax. I'm only here to invite you to come with me. It is not time for you yet, but soon. Once you are weaker. Very soon. And I can't wait to see what you will become."

"What are you doing here?" I managed to choke out.

"I came for you," he replied with a smile.

My heart skipped a beat. "No," I whispered. "You can't have me."

Drake's expression turned dark. "I already do."

"No," I said, louder this time, tears pricking at the corners of my eyes. "I won't give in."

Drake took a step closer. "But you know that's not true, don't you?" he said softly, his hand reaching out to stroke my cheek.

I flinched away from his touch, but he persisted, cupping my chin in his scorching hand. "You belong to me," he whispered in my ear.

Something inside me snapped, and all fear melted away in an instant. My hands balled into fists at my sides and I glared up at him with all the defiance I could muster.

"No, I don't."

Drake's grip on my chin tightened painfully. A snarl replaced his grin. He leaned down until our faces were only inches apart.

"You will never escape me," he growled before pushing me away. And I knew he hadn't meant him, but the Murk.

I stumbled backwards, trying to catch my breath as if I had been choking underwater.

The area suddenly filled with light. The scene switched to the view of a beautiful sunset from a mountaintop. I reached out, but I wasn't close enough. I thought that if I touched Drake, it would snap him out of it, releasing the Murk's hold on him like the Golden Child in that Eddie Murphy movie I once saw. The way the light surrounded him, he looked like an angel, but that too was a lie. That's what the Murk wanted. Him looking innocent and heavenly.

More importantly, though, he looked...happy. *What a facade.*

Curiosity filled me, but I was also confused. What did he mean about what I would become? Would I become like him, an avatar of the Murk? Never. I'd die first. And what did he mean about it not being time yet?

I had to reach him. Maybe he just needed to remember who he was. Trusting my instincts, I said his name. His real name. "Draven."

I stepped closer and reached out to touch him. His image flickered like a glitchy video game, his form momentarily disappearing and reappearing in quick succession. It was like watching a hologram malfunction, almost disappearing before popping back into focus.

"Draven, your sisters are free," I told him.

For a moment, he was himself. I saw it in his eyes. And then he spoke. "There is a place between angels and man," he said, "where heaven and hell collide. And it is there you will find the truth."

Immediately, he disappeared and so did the illusion. My breathing respite was over and I gasped for air again. I was suffocating, my life slipping away. I had to do something, but what? Somehow, I had to reach Draven. *Together... Together...* I fought the impulse to cry.

"Let go," the Murk demanded.

If I stopped fighting, it would win. What would happen to my family and friends? The pain was excruciating. *Fight Sheena! Remember who you are. I was created to...* It squeezed tighter. It enclosed me in a fiery embrace and tightened around my lungs like chains of smoke. *Created to...*

Dingy! I screamed inside.

CHAPTER 9

THEODORE

Mr. Meyer left us trying to understand the electricity connection and went upstairs to check on his wife.

"We've wasted another hour," said Chana. Dingy lay against her, sleeping peacefully. Suddenly, his eyes shot open, and he sat up. His chest heaved with his heavy breaths.

"Sheena," he said.

"It's okay, Dingy," I told him.

He shook his head and raised his arm, knocking my hand off of his shoulder. "No, I heard Sheena. She called my name."

"You were dreaming—"

He shook his head again and jumped up. All the while, he looked irritated that I suggested such a thing.

Suddenly, that warrior kid was back and before we could move, he dashed past us and out the side door of the house.

Mr. Meyer must have heard because he came flying down the stairs.

We ran after him and found Nana walking outside. Her hands were clasped in front of her, and her lips were moving, but she didn't acknowledge us.

"What's she doing?"

"She does that sometimes. She's praying a hedge of protection around the house," said Logan.

"Whatever that means," said Jasmine.

"Why did you stop? Someone go after him!" I yelled and looked behind me. Mr. Meyer was gone. I turned back toward Dingy's house and Mr. Meyer was across the yard, stopping Dingy. "How did he—"

Mrs. Meyer came to the door we had just left from. "Everyone, you need to hear this."

The twins were brought down to the family room. They looked better, but still like something from a B horror movie. Their voices were hoarse and kind of scared me.

Man up, Theodore, I thought as I looked around at everyone else to see how they were affected by it. No one else grimaced or anything, so I put on a facade of being unbothered. And it worked until they spoke again. They kind of croaked. The Murk had had them for years now. I was surprised they could talk at all. They were so frail that I wondered when they had last eaten before Nana fed them.

"It's our fault," one of the twins said, as the other nodded.

"Meaning what?" I asked. I didn't know which was which, Tiffany or Alexis, so I didn't bother with names.

"We were playing with fire. Tiffany and I had no idea what would happen."

Oh, that one is Tiffany.

"Then the Murk came for us, promising power, but it wasn't us that it was after," Tiffany added. "It wanted our brother, Draven..."

Alexis finished her sentence. "And the Murk knew if it took us, he would give himself to get back his little sisters."

"What did you do? I mean, why did it come after you in the first place?" asked Parker.

The twins glanced at each other, but didn't tell us. I figured whatever they were hiding was too bad to speak of, especially after seeing the candles and altar they built in that hidden room in their house.

Seren studied them. "Can you tell us what it did to you in there?" It was the question we all yearned to know.

One of the girls shook her head.

The silence, what they were not telling us, was just as bad as hearing their story. It left us to form our own ideas of what happened to them and what could be happening to Sheena.

Bradly sat at the edge of the sofa and shook her head. "No, we can't leave it at that." She looked around at all of us. "And before you guys start riding me about backing off, you know I'm right."

Corey patted his hand down, which I interpreted as him telling her to take it down a notch.

Bradly lowered her voice. "You have to tell us. We have to get our friend back. She rescued you. It's the least you can do."

Alexis glanced at her sister, who nodded. "The Murk gains strength from fear and anger—usually a result of someone's pain. Just like it wants to destroy the hope of kids because their hope is the strongest and the most unwavering, their fear and anger can also be amplified. Remember that chest?"

"You saw that?" I asked.

"We could see everything."

"Or at least feel it," said Tiffany.

"What chest?" asked Mrs. Meyer.

"The Murk tried to use it to—I don't know—absorb energy from Chana and Logan," I explained.

"Does it want to keep Sheena like it kept you?" asked Logan.

The twins shook their heads. Tiffany coughed harshly. Alexis held a towel to her sister's mouth and rubbed her back. "Not as long as it has our brother. It's going to drain her so it can strengthen to its full power. Forget everyone else. Sheena is all it needs."

"So it's going to kill her?" Corey asked.

Alexis nodded. "I think that was always the plan. And it's all our fault."

I balled my hands into fists so tightly that I thought my fingernails would cut through my palms.

Mrs. Meyer sat with her hand cupped over her mouth as she listened. If I didn't know any better, I'd bet she was trying to keep from screaming.

"Keep going. How is it your fault?" asked Corey.

"We led it to our brother. He became the Murk's avatar and as the darkness grew in him, he discovered Sheena." She cried. "Alexis, my eyes burn," she said, blinking hard.

Her twin held a damp towel to her eyes. "We didn't know what he was or even what a gleamer was. No one told us."

"No one told Sheena, either." It slipped. I didn't mean to say it. I could feel Mr. Meyer glaring at me.

"How did it even get to you?" asked Jasmine.

"Tiffany, hold the towel," her sister told her and turned to Jasmine. "Life is a series of roads leading you to destinations. Sometimes you take the wrong road."

"Sometimes you jump off a cliff," said her sister.

Then Tiffany leaned her head onto Alexis's. "I'm so sorry," she cried.

CHAPTER 10

THEODORE

The Murk destroyed any beauty these girls once had. My stomach coiled watching them, and I'd had enough of the conversation.

"Don't you think we need to tell their parents?" asked Jasmine. She was uneasy and chewing on a strand of her hair, which I hadn't seen her do in years.

"Yes, I want to go home," said the weaker twin.

"They're not going anywhere," said Mr. Meyer.

"We don't even know where their parents are, do we?" asked Ariel.

"That guy—the caretaker—he knows. We can ask him," I replied.

"He's still alive?" Alexis whispered.

Chana and I exchanged glances. I think she found the question just as bizarre as I did.

"Yeah, we can contact him," I told them and waited for a reaction.

"No," said Mr. Meyer. "As long as that thing has Sheena, they're staying right here."

"But their parents will want to know—"

"And they will. Get the information and they can come here," he replied with finality.

"While you were upstairs, we discussed which group would do what. It will cut the time down," said Corey. "As Theodore mentioned, we can get a hold of the caretaker of their house. He said he's seen someone who looks like Drake in the middle of the night, from time to time. I believe there is a time when Draven (his real name) is able to free himself just long enough to leave the info in that journal for Sheena—the only person who might free him. It makes sense. Maybe the caretaker has noticed a pattern of when he sees Draven. He could appear tonight. And if he does, we'll be there when he arrives."

"Is that where you just sent Justin?" I asked.

Corey nodded.

"I'm not hanging out there," said Parker.

"You'll do what needs to be done."

"We need to get to Phoenix's. Nana..." called Logan over Ariel's head.

She held her car keys up, already knowing we needed them. I hopped up, following Logan.

"Whoa, are you two safe alone together?" asked Parker.

"Somebody has to look after him," I replied. I followed Logan outside and climbed into the backseat of Corey's car. After the day's events, I didn't think I would ever sleep again. However, a few minutes after Corey, Logan, and I pulled away from Sheena's house, I opened my eyes to snoring coming from everyone. "Corey!" I exclaimed as I shook him.

Corey, slammed on the brakes. It was a miracle we didn't crash head-on into another vehicle.

"Man, what happened?" asked Logan from the front passenger seat.

"Did the Murk do that to us?" I asked.

"You can't blame everything on the Murk. It's not the master of sleep or anything," said Corey.

I leaned back against the headrest, looking out the window. It was weird not hearing from Sheena—even early in the morning. She thought of the oddest things at the oddest times and usually chose me to discuss them with. I would awaken hearing my phone chiming and lighting up with Sheena's name on the screen. A text alert of something crazy or random like, "Why do we wash fruit? Don't the pesticides get inside them too? Ditch the strawberries, Teddy." Then we would pull out our laptops, looking things up and texting the results of our research with lots of shocked emojis, laughing at each other until I demanded to go to sleep and Sheena's all, "Not until we figure this out," and suddenly she's hungry at 2 a.m.

We had snuck out before. Many times, actually. Even when we knew it was not safe to do so. I'd stand guard under her window, waiting until she emerged from the side, or back door, without setting off the alarm. And then we would run down the street to the lone twenty-four hour gas station. That was also back when Sheena still ate meat, so taquitos it was.

Someone's phone vibrated. Corey held his up.

"No texting and driving."

He looked back at me in the rearview mirror. "Seriously? Who do you think is calling right now other than one of the Knights?"

"Parent's maybe? Realizing we're not in our beds or up getting ready for school, or out walking the dog, or—"

"We get it," said Logan.

"It's Justin," said Corey.

CHAPTER II

JUSTIN

I closed my eyes and rubbed them. The gentle swaying of the truck, accompanied by the low rumble of the engine, was almost hypnotic. I struggled to stay awake. But that changed when I parked on the side of the road and stepped out into the cold air.

Bodhi followed me across the lawn of Draven's house and past the mangled for sale sign. The neighborhood was so quiet, it was impossible to believe anyone lived in the huge houses. Maybe they were owned by pro athletes or entertainers who weren't in town or someone who couldn't brave Michigan winters and went south like the ducks.

I wished I would have called Ma while we were at Sheena's house. I didn't want her to worry or to be the cause of her having a heart attack. She needed to live long enough for me to get drafted into the NFL, so I could buy her a proper house. Although, she liked to say, "I'm going to die in this house, Beanie. Don't waste your money. I'm never leaving."

"I'm glad we don't have to go back inside Draven's house," said Bodhi. "And I'm glad we didn't bring Parker."

"Why?"

"He's just so jittery all the time, even after becoming a Knight."

"True. He will man-up in a heartbeat though. Remember when he dressed as Sheena to fool the Murk?"

"Yeah, I have to admit, that was impressive. Those Murked-out boys could've beaten the snot out of him. I guess—"

"Shh..." I stopped walking around the pool and pointed. Bodhi stopped too. He couldn't go any further. My other arm was stretched in front of his chest, holding him back. "The doors..."

French doors stretched across the entire backside of the house on the first floor, and they were open.

I reached inside my coat pocket for my phone and held it in front of me.

Bodhi pushed it down. "What are you doing? Taking a selfie?"

"No, recording all of this," I said and turned the camera, filming. "Come on," I whispered.

We walked in single file, trailing behind the main house and heading towards the smaller cottage of the caretaker. It shared the same design as the larger house with its wooden panels and shutters. The caretaker had cleared a path leading to the cottage, revealing the slate tiles beneath the snow.

I felt good about seeing the old man again. He recognized me, after all. I only hoped I would be successful at getting the necessary information from him. It was a nice change of pace to not just be seen as the muscle of the group because of my size. Corey had put me in charge of this part of the mission. I wouldn't let him down.

As we approached a door (I couldn't tell if it was the front, side, or back door), I slowed. The closer we got, I could see that it, too, was open. I stopped walking and Bodhi walked right into me and fell back.

"What the heck—"

I turned with a finger to my lips and pulled him up.

We both faced the door and stood there, staring at it. Finally, Bodhi nudged me. I swallowed hard and gripped my phone tightly, my mind racing with thoughts. What was I worried about? It wasn't like the empty home up front. Someone actually lived here. Of course, people left their doors wide open in the winter to let some air in. Not.

On the door was a handwritten note: Gone out for a bit. Back soon.

My shoulders dropped. I was relieved. The man had gone out and forgotten to close the door behind him. Maybe he had left in a hurry. Things happen. He may have needed something from a home improvement store. They open early. Nails or something. Or maybe there was someone else inside his house. I tried to push those thoughts away and focus on the task at hand. I wouldn't be a Knight if I didn't make sure everything was okay. The guy was pretty old. What if he didn't get a chance to leave because he had a stroke or something?

I slowly stepped forward and pushed on the door. "Hello... Mr.... Mr. Caretaker? Are you home?"

Silence was the only response. I hesitated for a moment, then took a deep breath and entered the house. Bodhi and I exchanged a brief glance. I think he sensed that something was off, too, and followed close behind me. As I walked, I looked back, seeing he was now filming. "Mr. Caretaker?" I called out again, my voice barely above a whisper. "I was hoping to talk to you about the house."

Still no answer. I took short steps around the room, my eyes darting around for any sign of life. Even though the sun was rising, with the curtains closed, I could barely make out the shape of a couch in front of me and a small table to my left. To my right was a kitchen area, but it was too dark to make out any details. A vase with dead flowers sat on a table beside the door.

Suddenly, there was a noise from upstairs—a creaking floorboard followed by the sound of something heavy being dragged across the room. I pointed up. Bodhi shook his head and banged his forearms together. That was his way of saying we needed the rest of the Knights of the Gleam. I shook my head and headed for the stairs.

"Mr. Caretaker?" I called out again, louder this time, wishing I knew the guy's actual name.

Bodhi slapped his forehead and slammed his finger to his lips, telling me to shut up.

"Stay here," I whispered. "I'll go check it out."

He shook his head and grabbed my arm, as if he could hold me back. I pulled away and climbed the steps, trying to stay as quiet as possible, hoping I wouldn't step on any creaky floorboards that might give us away. Each step felt like a small victory.

At the top, I stood and waited, my eyes adjusting to the darkness. Then I noticed a dark shape on the floor, on the side of the bed of the loft. My heart raced, as Bodhi walked up beside me, his breathing quickening.

"What is that?"

CHAPTER 12

THEODORE

"Pull over," I told Corey.

He drove over to the curb and placed the call on speaker. "Yo, what happened?"

"You're not going to believe this," said Justin.

"Try me."

"Well, I expected to knock on the caretaker's door and say, 'Hey, Mister. Remember us?' and he'd say something like, 'To what do I owe this unexpected honor?'"

"Justin, just tell us what happened," I yelled.

"He's dead," came Bodhi's voice.

"No way. Are you sure?" asked Corey.

"Is this our fault?" asked Justin.

"No, I think it was a matter of time. He knew too much. The Murk knew we would get information from him."

"What in tarnation?" said Justin.

"What? What is it?" I exclaimed. We were all accustomed to Justin's 'what in tarnations.'

"Just get here."

"We're heading to Phoenix's," said Logan.

"Not anymore."

We sped to Draven's house, and Corey griped the entire way about wasting time. When we arrived, we didn't bother parking up the block with Justin's car like we did the last time we came—when Sheena was with us. We parked right in the circular driveway.

A shoveled path led us around the back of the house, where we ran straight to the caretaker's cottage and stopped at the door. "Justin!" Corey called.

"Up here!"

Corey stepped inside first. Then Logan and me. All of the curtains were drawn. We shone the lights from our phones around the living area that opened to a kitchen with floating stairs at the back wall.

"We're upstairs," said Bodhi.

Our steps were loud as we hurried up to them. I stopped on the landing of the loft. A lone lamp shone on the side of the bed, gave off just enough light to illuminate a clump of clothing on the floor.

As I got closer, I saw it wasn't a clump of clothing at all. I covered my mouth from the shock of what I saw and my nose from the stench. "How were you able to stay up here?" I asked through my fingers.

"It wasn't easy," said Justin. "We thought we should go through his things."

"Good idea," said Corey.

"Good thinking," Logan said at the same time.

I knelt closer. "It looks like the life has been sucked right out of him. Literally. What is this stuff all over him?" I picked up a piece.

"Don't touch him."

The thin black paper instantly disintegrated. "It's like soot or something."

"Just like what was on the twins," said Corey.

"Did you find anything?" asked Logan.

Bodhi held out his hand. "He knew we were coming back. Either us or Sheena. Look at this. He left this note for her."

"Where did you get this?"

"I took it from him. His hand was balled in a fist."

"So you opened it?"

"Yeah, I could see it clutching something."

"What I think happened is that he had it in his hand when the Murk came for him. Maybe he grabbed it at the last minute. Bodhi gently pried it out and unfolded it," said Justin.

I wrinkled my nose. "Gross."

"Yeah, it was."

"Well what does it say?" I asked.

Bodhi stepped closer. On the paper was a hastily scribbled message. "'We are with you. Hide the key. May your vision be true.'"

"Key? What key?" Corey asked.

"That key," said Justin, pointing.

Bodhi held up a small, silver key with an intricate design etched into it. It looked ancient. "It was taped to the back of his dresser drawer."

We all stared at it in silence.

"All right, I know you're mesmerized by this thing," said Corey, "but we need to keep moving. Let's go."

"Does anyone hear ticking?" asked Bodhi. "Like something tapping on metal."

"He keeps saying that," said Justin. "But I don't hear it."

I shook my head.

"Did you find anything the key could unlock?" Logan asked while shining the light from his phone over it."

"Nope."

I scratched my head. "There has to be something here. It must be important, or why would he hide it? It may help Sheena."

"No doubt," said Corey. "But if the Murk did this, for all we know it's watching us right now. We should go."

We all agreed and headed down the stairs. I was the last to leave, glancing around the room one final time for anything that might have something to do with Sheena. As I did, the caretaker's body suddenly illuminated. The ash flicked away into sparks of light.

My mouth dropped, as I stared at the spot where what was left of his body lay. My breathing quickened, like I had just run a marathon. "G-g-get back up here!" I stuttered.

The Knights bounded up the stairs.

"What in tarnation?" asked Justin. "Where did he go?"

CHAPTER 13

LOGAN

I had never heard Theodore sound as terrified as he did at that moment. His words were like a guttural scream, reverberating through my bones. Without hesitation, I raced up the stairs.

Justin stood at the top beside Theodore, his normally strong frame trembling and his eyes wild.

I stepped onto the landing, and as I did, I saw the spirit form of the old man—the caretaker, rise and leave with angels, just as Sheena said she saw happen with my father. He met my gaze and nodded before fading away. His faint whisper rang in my ears: "May your vision be true."

I stared at the wall he disappeared through, my mind racing to make sense of why I had been allowed to witness his crossover. Someone grabbed my arm, and I jumped as a tear rolled down my cheek. I quickly wiped it away.

"How did his body just disappear like that?" Corey looked into my eyes. "What did you see?"

"He wasn't up here," said Theodore. "He didn't see what I saw."

"Just now," said Corey, ignoring Theodore. "What was it?"

Everyone waited. Corey nodded, as if he understood. He held the same expression of awe, and for a moment I almost thought Corey had seen him too.

"Theodore, what did you see?" I asked.

"H-his body lit up like he had neon inside of him and then flickered away like fireflies in the night."

I nodded. "But you couldn't see what happened next."

"What?" asked Theodore.

"I saw him crossover."

We stared at each other for a long moment.

"We need to go."

"Wait," said Theodore. "Yes, he disappeared, but that's only part of what I wanted you to see." He pointed. "Look at the floor."

"Hold on..." I knelt and jabbed my finger towards the small indentation in the wooden floorboards. "Does that key fit in there?"

Corey bent down and inspected it before shaking his head.

"No, it doesn't fit," Theodore said. "But that's not the point. Look closer."

I examined the floorboards. The wood was worn, but there was something different about one of the planks. It was slightly raised, as if it had been propped up from underneath.

I reached for the board and lifted it up. "Run!" I screamed.

CHAPTER 14
THEODORE

Corey and I were hanging over Logan's shoulder when he lifted the floorboard. The bomb ticked, like a clock, but didn't tell how many minutes or seconds we had left. *How did someone know how long it would take us to get here and that we would still be here?*

Thank goodness the cottage was small. There were only a few steps from the staircase to the front door. "Go, go, go!" Corey yelled as he pushed me and Logan in front of him and we bolted out of there.

When the bomb went off, we were running past the swimming pool with our backs to the cottage.

The explosion behind us sent a shockwave rippling through the air.

I could feel the heat on my back as we ran. The force of the blast lifted us off our feet and propelled us forward.

I landed hard on the ground, my ears ringing and a searing pain pulsing in my back. My vision blurred, and it took a moment for me to regain my bearings. When I finally did, I found Corey lying beside me, groaning.

"Logan!" I shouted.

He was lying face down a few feet away from us, his body limp and unmoving. Panic set in as I crawled over to him and placed two fingers on his neck and checked for a pulse like I had learned in CPR class.

He was alive.

I rolled him over, seeing his coat was singed and torn.

"Logan, can you hear me?" I asked, shaking him gently.

His eyes squeezed tight and then opened. He gasped, and his face twisted in pain. "I'm okay," he said weakly. "Just a little banged up."

"Are *you* okay, Theodore?" Corey groaned.

"I'm fine," I said, trying to sound confident. "Just a scratch."

But the truth was, I was in excruciating pain. I could feel the blood seeping from a wound on my leg.

We were relieved to find that Justin and Bodhi had come through the explosion unscathed. But Justin wouldn't stop repeating, "Someone wants us dead, like literally wants us dead."

"It's more likely they wanted to make sure there was nothing left of the caretaker or whatever he was hiding here," said Bodhi.

"Let's get out of here," I told them and helped Logan to his feet. But Logan couldn't take his eyes off of Corey.

"Stop," he said.

"Stop for what? We need to go," Corey replied, his voice urgent. "The person who set that bomb could still be around."

"He's right, Logan," I agreed. "We needed to move, and fast." With me supporting him on one side and Corey on the other, we stumbled towards the car, following Justin and Bodhi.

Corey opened the passenger side door, and Logan held to the door like it was a crutch.

"You're bleeding," said Corey, staring at my pant leg.

I glanced at it. "Yeah, I know, but I thought we were in a hurry."

"We need to see how bad it is." He knelt and rolled up my jeans. I didn't look.

"Here," said Logan, handing Corey his scarf.

Corey tied it tightly around my leg, making me grimace. "That should help stop the flow, but I think you're going to need stitches." He motioned to Justin and he and Bodhi hurried up the block to his truck. "Let's go."

"No," said Logan, turning to Corey.

"Dude, do you not hear those sirens? How are you going to explain what we are doing here?" I asked.

"How did we survive that?" asked Logan.

I carefully sat in the backseat and put my leg in the car. "What are you talking about? We ran. And just in time, too."

Logan shook his head. "We're not that fast. We were too close. I felt my body being pushed forward."

I reached for my seatbelt. "Yeah, from the blast—the pressure of it bursting out."

Corey closed my door and went around to the drivers side and got behind the wheel. He was about to shift the car into drive when Logan grabbed his hand, stopping him from shifting.

"How long have you known you are a gleamer?"

CHAPTER 15

THEODORE

Logan's question hung heavy in the air, as sirens grew louder in the distance.

"Wait a minute. Did I hear him right? Is it true, Corey? You're a gleamer?" I exclaimed, as I sat erect in the seat, ignoring the throbbing coming from my leg. "Does Cameron know? Does Sheena know?"

From the rearview mirror, I watched Corey's eyes widen in surprise. "What are you talking about?" he asked, glancing first at Logan and then over the seat at me.

"You heard me," Logan said, his voice anxious. "I felt it just before the bomb went off. It was like a shockwave, and I could feel my own gleam pushing back against it, helping it save us."

Corey shook his head.

"Come on, don't play dumb," said Logan. "I saw you. I glanced back. Your arms were raised. And some type of force field spread around us. You're a gleamer, just like me. You can control energy."

My heart raced as I listened to Logan's words, repeating them in my head.

Corey continued shaking his head. I don't know if he thought he was convincing us, but it wasn't working. "I don't know what you're talking about," he said, shifting the car into gear. "But we can't stay here. We need to get out of this neighborhood, fast."

Justin's truck pulled up beside us, and he rolled down the window with Bodhi leaning forward, looking inside our car. "What the heck are y'all waiting on? Let's go!"

The sirens grew louder by the minute, and I knew we needed to put as much distance as we could between ourselves and that property.

We backed out of the driveway, and Justin followed us up the road. After a few minutes, a fire truck blared its horn and raced through an intersection without slowing down. Every so often, Corey eyed me in the rearview mirror, seeing me watching him.

"You're like me, aren't you?" Logan asked again, looking straight ahead. When Corey didn't respond, he turned to him.

"I..." Corey hesitated and then exhaled heavily and relaxed in his seat. "Fine. Yes, I am." He looked over the seat at me. "Cameron doesn't know."

"Eyes on the road!" I shouted. "Ha! I know what this is. You guys are funny, but this is no time for jokes." I pointed back and forth at them. "I see what you two are doing. How long have you had this planned? 'Let's prank Theodore. We'll be laughing for weeks about it.' Yeah, try that on Parker. *He* would actually fall for it."

Corey stopped at a red light, took a deep breath, and closed his eyes. I watched him through the rearview mirror. "Dude, open your eyes. The joke's over."

When he opened them again, they were shining with an otherworldly light.

I hopped up in my seat. "What the freak?"

"Calm down, Theodore," said Logan. "Corey, how long have you known?"

"After I met Sheena—after I helped her that day at that apartment complex in the Heights." He glanced at Logan. "When we saved her from your father."

Logan only nodded.

"Is that why you changed—why you went from juvenile thug to class president overnight?" I asked.

Corey drove through the intersection without a response.

"Well, in case you're worried. You haven't lost all of your thugdum."

Both Corey and Logan let out a small chuckle and a hand flew over the seat at me, which I dodged and looked behind us seeing headlights flashing.

I patted Corey's headrest with my fist. "Something's up with Justin. Slow down."

Justin flashed his lights again. Corey pulled the car over, and we all hopped out. I limped over to where they stood behind the car. "What's going on?"

"It's Ma," said Justin.

Suddenly, rings, chirps, and chimes came from all of us.

"This can't be good," I said, knowing we were all thinking it.

Everyone took their phone from their pockets. "My mother," said Bodhi. I have to go.

I looked at my phone. "Something's wrong with my mother too. Take me home."

"If anything, I need to get you to the hospital or to Ariel." Corey's phone rang, and he answered it. "Hey, what's up? I'm working. Yes. What happened to her?"

"Something's not right here," Logan whispered. "We can't just all go home."

My phone vibrated, and I checked the texts:

> Bradly: Why won't you guys pick up?
> Something is wrong with my mom. I can't
> stay here.

> Teila: I'm walking home. I'm not afraid.

"Are you guys seeing these texts?" I asked.
Logan showed me his phone.

> Ariel: Where are you? Something happened to my father.

"Back to Sheena's house," Logan exclaimed.
"No," said Bodhi.
"Yes, Listen. All of our mothers at the same time? Either this is another one of the Murk's tricks or it's attacking our families to get to us," said Corey.

I tried to dissolve the worry building in me as I processed Corey's words. The Murk had always been relentless in its pursuit to destroy us. It fed on chaos, and now it seemed to have found a new way to torment us by targeting our families. "Why, though?"

"It means the Murk is threatened by us. Think about it. Logan doesn't have a parent. He didn't get a call, other than Ariel. No offense, man."

"It's okay. It's just a fact."

"The Murk knows we're working to free Sheena, and it's trying to distract us. That thing knows!" Corey exclaimed while pounding one fist on top of the other.

"It knows what?"

"Think about it. Why would it go to these lengths? It knows Sheena only has so much time. And..."

"And what?" I asked.

"And it knows we have a chance a freeing her."

"I understand that, but I can't take a chance that something might be happening to Ma," said Justin. "What do we do?"

"Ma... That's it. She's a descendant of the City of Gleamers. Have all the families and the City of Gleamers go to Sheena's house. They'll be safe there," said Logan.

"Yeah...Nana's hedge of protection, right?" I asked. "Are you sure that works?"

TIME REMAINING: 18 HOURS

CHAPTER 16

JUSTIN

"**M**a!" I called as I jumped over the first two stairs of the porch and landed on the last. My hands shook as I tried to get my house key into the keyhole, scraping it on the door. *Chill*, I told myself. *She's fine. You know she is. As crazy as she is, she would scare the Murk away, if anything.*

"Ma!" I repeated, finally unlocking and pushing open the door. Bodhi ran to the back of the house and I ran to her bedroom. "Ma!"

Suddenly, a scream came from the other side of the house.

My breath caught in my throat. "Please God, no!" I whispered and shot off.

Bodhi knelt on the floor, frantically rubbing his eyes. "I can't see," he cried, "She maced me."

Ma stood over him, holding a spray bottle. I ran to her and picked her up in the air.

"Beanie, what in tarnation? Put me down, boy!"

I carefully set her down as Bodhi stood, opened one eye, and went to the sink.

"What kind of poison did you spray on me?"

"Stop your whining. It's just my tonic. All natural. I use it to clean everything."

Bodhi now smelled of cinnamon, frankincense, and other oils.

"Ma, you can't go around spraying people with that stuff! And go put your teeth in."

"I was minding my business, is what I was doing, and he ran in here without me letting him in the house. He said, 'Ma!'"

"And your reaction was to squirt him?"

"Beanie, don't make me get my belt. I don't have to defend what I do in my own house. What's going on with you?" She looked at me hard and touched a residual tear on my cheek. "You're too big to be crying like an infant." Her voice softened. "Ma's all right." She patted my shoulder and set the spray bottle down. "Let me go and put my wig on so you can tell me what's happened."

"And your teeth," I said.

Bodhi dried his eyes with a dish towel and turned off the running water in the sink.

"Are you okay, man?"

"Yeah, but I thought your grandmother was going to assault me with a flying kick or something." Bodhi cringed and shook his head. "What is she doing up so early?"

I shrugged, "Ma is always up early. She says that her job is never done and I guess that includes cleaning, too. Come on, now we know Corey was right. Those texts are fake and there's nothing wrong with our parents."

"That's a relief," said Bodhi. "Wait, when did the Murk get the ability to do that?"

Minutes later, Ma had pulled her curly black wig over her stocking cap and put her teeth in. "Talk," she said sternly, while motioning for us to sit down in the living room.

We relayed the events of the past few hours and ended with Logan showing us his phone and then heading back to Sheena's house, while we came to check on *her* as quickly as possible.

Ma listened intently, not saying much but nodding her head now and then. When we finished, we waited for her response.

Finally, Ma slapped the coffee table hard, and we jumped. "Ha! That thing is slick. I didn't send any text. I've never sent a text a day in my life. I do things the old way. It's trying to rattle you." She pointed. "It knows it can." She looked at me as if she were looking over invisible glasses. "How does it know?"

"How am I supposed to know?"

Ma shook her head. "You've shown it. You kids react to everything. It knows that more than anything, there are people that you love and if it can get to them, or make you think it can, it can control you."

"It's not controlling us."

"Oh, no?"

"Not at all."

"Are you supposed to be here right now?"

Bodhi and I looked at each other with our mouths open. "We were supposed to go to Sheena's house," I replied.

Ma fell back against the sofa, laughing. "Knights of the Gleam. Ha!"

"Okay, okay. You don't have to laugh at us."

Ma stood. "Okay, Beanie. I've got things to do. The City of Gleamers are meeting. I heard tell there's some people that need our protecting."

"That's what we came to tell you."

"Well, you're late."

CHAPTER 17
THEODORE

"**D**ad! Mom!" I yelled as I ran and opened the side door of the house. If the Murk hurt either of them I was going to—going to... I didn't know what I was going to do, but something.

"Hey, hey, what's wrong?" My mother's voice was as soothing as a warm blanket. She came down the stairs in her robe, maneuvering a pin curl back under her satin bonnet. "Where have you been? Did the coach call an early practice?"

"Are you okay? Is Dad?" I asked, as I clasped her hands.

"Ooo, your hands are freezing. Of course he's okay. He's sleeping in today. His alarm should go off soon. Talk to me. What is this about?"

I looked behind me. Logan nodded and backed out of the house. He only came in with me to make sure everything was okay. Corey would drive him back to Sheena's. For the moment, I was disappointed in myself for doubting he had Sheena's back.

"Teddy, is that blood on your pants?"

I paused before answering. My mother and Sheena were the only two people in the world who called me Teddy. I would give anything to hear Sheena say it again.

"Yes, it's blood. I'm okay though."

"But you're limping."

I hadn't told her about being a Knight of the Gleam, as Chana had suggested, or about anything concerning gleamers and the Murk.

I glanced down at my leg. The adrenaline that had been pumping through me had masked the pain until now. My jeans were torn, and blood was visible through the scarf Corey had tied around it.

"It's just a scratch," I lied.

My mother wasn't convinced. "Let me take a look at it," she said and gestured for me to sit on the couch. "Are you going to tell me where you've been? I checked your room before I heard you calling. Your bed hasn't been slept in." Her voice was even toned. She was trying to remain calm, and I appreciated it.

"That's what I want to talk to you about."

"Hold that thought." She hurried away and came back with a plastic container filled with first aid supplies. "Go ahead, I'm listening."

"I was... I mean, I know I should have told you this a while ago. There's no good reason why I didn't. I-I guess I was afraid. Afraid you wouldn't believe me and—afraid you would." I took a deep breath and exhaled. "My friends and I are fighting for the hope of the world against a dark force called the Murk. We are called the Knights of the Gleam," I said, as I tried to steady my voice.

Her face paled slightly as she listened to me and stopped moving.

"I promise I'm not lying to you. An-an angel made us Knights." I looked down at the bandage she placed on my leg. "I need you and Dad to come with me right now to Sheena's house."

"For what? I think I'm missing something," she said. "Your father is about to go to work. You have school today. Why—"

I cut her off and tried my best to keep my voice even. "Because you're my parents. The Murk may come after you. You will be protected there."

I expected her to laugh or to dismiss me as crazy, but instead, she listened intently.

"I know this is all confusing and sounds nuts, but it has to do with the City of Gleamers."

My mother's eyes widened at the mention of them. "What about them?"

"What about them? You mean you know about them? About gleamers?"

My mother hesitated for a moment before speaking. She nodded solemnly. "Yes. My grandmother used to tell me stories when I was a child. She said they were protectors of the light and fought against the darkness."

I nodded my head vigorously. "Yes, that's it! The City of Gleamers. It's not just a rumor, it's real. And the Murk wants to destroy them, and us, but we're fighting to protect it and all of humanity."

My mother hesitated for a moment, biting her lip while looking away from me.

"Mom, please. Just tell me."

"People who have lived here in Muskegon for generations know all about it," my father said from the stairs. "About gleamers and the Murk."

"The Murk has taken Sheena."

My mother gasped and shot up from her seat. My father ran down the rest of the stairs. "You've seen it?" he asked.

"It's the reason I've been in therapy." I could feel the knots in my stomach starting to loosen as I realized my parents believed me. "We need to go."

"Go where?" ask my father.

I realized he hadn't heard that part of the conversation. "Sheena's house. You will be safe there."

"Safe?" he asked.

I didn't want to say it. They were already about to start freaking out. "I want you to come with me because you trust me. That's all. Just trust me."

"Hurry, get dressed," he told my mother.

In minutes, we were driving to Sheena's house. My mother listened intently, occasionally asking questions for clarification. But not once did they get on my case for hiding all of this from them or for sneaking out of the house at all hours of the night.

From the backseat of the car, I watched my parents, as I recounted all of my adventures as a Knight of the Gleam. Glances were exchanged between them, silent acknowledgments of an unspoken understanding. My mom reached between the front seats and squeezed my hand, a small but powerful gesture.

I had to hand it to Seren, our newest unofficial team member. She knew what she was talking about when she said, "You need to tell them. You need that support. You may not believe it, but life becomes a little easier when they know." She was right. The weight of fighting against the Murk held me down like an anchor at the bottom of the sea. But opening up to my folks lifted me just enough to break the surface and catch a breath. Soon, thoughts of Sheena flooded in, hitting me like a massive wave, slamming me back to the ocean floor. It left me in a weird place, teetering between faith and doubt. I couldn't escape the internal struggle.

The drive to Sheena's house was faster than I would have liked. Now that I had opened up. I didn't want to stop. But maybe I had said enough. I didn't want to overwhelm them.

So many cars lined Sheena's block that we had to park around the corner.

Nana wore an apron and greeted us with a smile as we walked through the side entrance of the house. From the hall, the kitchen smelled and sounded like a breakfast restaurant. Dishes clanking and voices filling the air. Nana was a perfect hostess, strolling through each room, making sure everyone was comfortable and didn't need anything. She amazed me at how she managed to conceal any hint of the pain she felt about the Murk taking Sheena.

My parents greeted the other parents that were in the family room. The City of Gleamers sat in the living room. They were the oldest gleamers in the city—the descendants of the children who were hidden underground back when all the inhabitants of Muskegon were gleamers, and the Murk sought to kill them and burn down the town.

All around me, people were eating. Bacon passed by on a plate, and then biscuits. I was hungry. From the next plate someone carried by, I grabbed a slice of toast. I walked through the rooms looking for the Knights and found all except two. Then Logan came from upstairs and I stopped him. "Where is Cameron?"

"He and Quincy still aren't picking up and haven't come back."

"That's crazy. I think we all need to regroup downstairs."

Logan whistled and circled a finger in the air.

Every head turned to him. Nana, with lips pursed, placed her hand on her hip.

"Oh, sorry about the whistle."

The Knights bounded down the stairs and crowded around the fireplace.

"My mom already knew about the City of Gleamers," I told them.

"Mine had heard of them," said Parker.

"Mine knew too," said Teila.

"That's because they are all originally from Muskegon. The whole city used to be gleamers," Ariel reminded them.

"I was so glad to tell them about gleamers and everything when they already knew," said Bodhi. We went there after picking up Ma. Do you know she maced me?

"Mine was all, 'This explains a lot,'" said Jasmine.

Suddenly, while listening to everyone, it hit me—the truth about our ancestry—our shared history. My mother already knew about the City of Gleamers; she just never knew that I knew about them until now. All our families were connected somehow; Corey's grandparents had moved away from Muskegon after their daughter had gone missing decades ago; Logan's family had disappeared from here shortly after his birth; Parker said his family had left Muskegon when he was little, but came back and never really said why they left in such a hurry…it all made sense now. We were supposed to come together.

"So what's next? What are we doing? Because all of this has taken up so much time. We're about seven hours in and I am about to collapse," said Bradly.

Bodhi studied her. "Time… Wow. I can't believe we didn't figure that out until an hour ago."

"Figure out what?" asked Bradly.

"The Murk knows how much time Sheena has. It's doing things to use up that time. We've gotta speed this up."

"I think I know a way," said Logan.

TIME REMAINING: 14 HOURS

CHAPTER 18

LOGAN

Before moving in with the Meyers, my life was nothing but secrets. Very similar to Sheena's. I was constantly being shuffled between foster homes, and for a time, didn't know who my real family was. Then I found out I was a gleamer, and there was yet another thing I had to hide. I had become accustomed to keeping things to myself; living as a walking mystery. With my history, it should have been easier to not tell the Knights what I had discovered regarding the caretaker—something only Sheena or I would understand. As his words echoed, "May your vision be true," a scene flashed before my eyes: an owl and then a place, but I didn't know where. A fleeting glimpse of a woman clutching a key. It happened so fast, I questioned if I really saw it.

"I'll be right back." I told Theodore.

"But you said you knew a way to speed things up. Aren't you going to fill us in?"

"Not yet."

"Then should we head to Phoenix's?"

"Yes," said Corey.

"No," I countered. Even though I wanted Corey to act as leader of the Knights, the fact remained that *I* was the leader and not him, so they had to listen to me and stay put. "As soon as I'm back, and every parent is here. In the meantime, let's compile all the information we have." *That should keep them busy.*

I hurried to Uncle Jonas, ignoring the grumbles behind me.

"Where's the journal?" I whispered, as he poured coffee into several brown mugs.

"You need it?"

"I just remembered something. Can I see it for a minute?" My eyes shifted to the map sprawled out on the kitchen island, pages taped together with areas highlighted in pink, orange, and yellow.

Uncle Jonas noticed my interest in the map. "I printed it from Sheena's laptop. It pinpoints areas where the Murk's presence has been detected. Look at this. Do you notice anything interesting?"

I looked closer. Lines were drawn from highlighted circles around Detroit, Lansing, Benton Harbor and Grand Rapids. My finger traced to the single point where they all met. "Muskegon Heights?"

Uncle Jonas nodded and handed me the journal. He leaned against the counter. "What are you looking for in it?"

"I-I just remembered something."

He looked suspicious at first, or maybe just curious about what I was up to, but he didn't press further. Perhaps he trusted me. I hoped he did, despite not being able to save Sheena from the Murk.

I ran upstairs to my bedroom. Probably the only room in the house with no one in it. Voices came from down the hall, as I closed the door and walked around my bed. I opened the journal. Sitting wasn't an option. If I let my guard down for even a moment, exhaustion would takeover and I'd be asleep in seconds. I flipped through the pages until I found the one that confused me once, but now made sense. Without hesitation, I grabbed my phone, found the name I was looking for, and hit the call button.

"Took you long enough, kiddo."

"Hey, Aunt Aria. Did you know I was going to call or something?"

"Something like that."

"Where are you?"

"Outside your door."

"Stop playing." I had been pacing on the other side of my bed and suddenly stopped. No sounds came from outside my door. I walked over and opened it. There she was, looking like an older version of Sheena, without the purple hair. I hugged her hard and quickly backed up. "I'm sorry. I don't know why I just did that."

"You must be really happy to see me."

"That and you look so much like Sheena, I mean she looks like you." Her eyes were red. "You've been crying."

"Haven't we all." It wasn't a question.

"What are you doing here?" I asked.

"The same reason everyone else is here." She glanced at the journal in my hand. "What's going on?"

"I wanted— I mean— Umm..."

She waited patiently for me to ask.

"It's about a sticky note I found in this journal. It's Sheena's handwriting..."

Aunt Aria lifted a brow and came closer. "And..."

"Can you show me the last thing you showed Sheena?"

She didn't respond.

I squinted and raised my shoulders. "If I'm not being intrusive," I added and braced myself for the opposite reaction of what I wanted.

"Aunt Aria?" I snapped my fingers in front of her face and she grinned. "Whoa!" I exclaimed and looked around.

Suddenly, I felt like Dorothy in the Wizard of Oz, though I'd never admit to my boys that I even knew what took place in that film. *We're not in Kansas anymore, Toto,* I thought, as everything in the room melded together around me into a kaleidoscope of colors.

"Will you take the journey, even though you know where it leads?"

I looked around for where the booming voice had come from. Seconds later, the phrase repeated. I got the feeling it wouldn't stop until I responded. "Uh, I guess..." *Was this what Sheena experienced?* She never gave details about Aunt Aria's gleamer gift or her journeys with her—only that she was some sort of traveler. She righted the wrongs of the past. If that was true, why couldn't we right what happened to Sheena?

In seconds, I stood in a vast desert. A white owl floated above in the bright sky. *That's the owl.* Its wings emitted a gentle white glow, and with each flutter, it released twinkles of gold.

I stood there waiting and wiping sweat from my forehead. The sun beat down on me like I was really there. "What does this have to do with Sheena?" I finally exclaimed. "What am I doing here?" I hadn't even had a conversation with Aunt Aria. *She just chose some random place to send me?*

"Walk," I heard.

I lifted my arms. "Which way?" There was no response, so I walked straight ahead. *This was a bad idea. This desert has nothing to do with saving Sheena. What's wrong with me? I should have told her, "Take me back to the moment we decided to go to that trailer park." But she didn't give me a chance. My bedroom, the Meyer home and everyone in it, just disappeared.*

In the haze of the day, I could just barely make out something in the distance and quickened my pace toward it. What I thought were animals moving about were people.

As I got closer, I realized it was an excavation site. A tall woman with blonde hair noticed me and smiled warmly.

It's her! The woman the caretaker showed me!

"You're finally here!" She hurried over. "You must be Elizabeth's nephew."

"I guess," was all I could think of to say.

"Oh, you're a funny one. We like that. We need more of that here."

She motioned toward some tents not far away. "Set your camp over there." She was looking behind me.

I turned, seeing that a caravan followed me. "Where did they come from?"

She laughed. "You sure don't travel light, I see."

I stared at her, dumbfounded.

"I'm Professor Pembly. Welcome, young man! You must be feeling disoriented right now, but you'll get used to all of this soon enough." She fanned herself and placed her hands on her hips. "It's not easy dealing with the heat during the day and then the cold nights. But it is all so very interesting—gaining insight into ancient civilizations."

Professor Pembly extended her hand, and I shook it slowly. *What could this possibly have to do with Sheena?*

She nodded, her face pleasant, and kept right on talking. "Your family has been involved in this research for ages now, and I'm glad they recruited you to help with the project. I mean, they *are* funding it." She whispered the last part, as if there were someone else close enough to hear it. "We need someone who is capable of detecting unusual occurrences and who can document them accurately as they happen."

Detect? Unusual occurrences?

Her hand graced her lips (cracked from dehydration) as if she were overly excited about something. "I'm sure that you would like to rest up after your journey, so that you are alert tomorrow morning, but I have something to show you."

She grabbed my arm, leading me inside the excavation site. "We were just about to uncover something special here," she said. "I can sense its power even while it's buried beneath the sand."

Power? Wait, she said sense. How?

We stopped at a large stone structure that had been unearthed. It was covered in intricate carvings that reminded me of a child's drawing. The stick figures told some kind of story.

"Look at these symbols. I bet you didn't expect to find this when you arrived," Professor Pembly said, without looking away from the structure. Then she pointed to one of the carvings which showed two identical stick people holding hands, one larger than the other, and a bolt of lightning between them.

"It means strength," she finally said after a few moments had passed in silence. "That symbol represents the connection between two people, specifically two gleamers."

She knows about gleamers? What is happening? Why did Aunt Aria bring me here?

"Here. I wasn't going to show you this until tomorrow, but I think it's important," she said solemnly, as she dusted off and then handed me a small device that looked like a key made out of metal and stone combined into an intricate design. "It requires two people who are connected through the gleam to use it properly."

Connected through the gleam? Why does this resemble the key the caretaker had? If the stone was removed, the key could be altered by a blacksmith or something, then they would be identical.

I pretended to admire it and handed it back to her. Professor Pembly held up the key as if needing the sunlight to analyze it.

She suddenly looked past me, and her body stiffened. "Phillip, do not say a word," she whispered and I turned to faced whoever was coming. She stepped in front of me, shielding me behind her.

"What's happening up here?" he asked gruffly. "Did you find anything?"

"No," she replied, as she pressed her hand into mine. My fingers graced her palm for only a moment. It was like touching Ariel. *She's a gleamer.* I took the key from her and placed it in my pocket without him noticing.

The man stormed forward, and pushed Professor Pembly aside. He wore a turban, and his skin was very tanned. He looked into my eyes and brought his face so close that I had to lean back some to stop his nose from touching mine.

Hide your gleam, I told myself. I don't know how I knew, but I was certain he knew exactly what a gleamer was and that I might be one. But I wasn't me. Was the boy a gleamer?

"You should not be here," the man said, his lips curled into a permanent snarl.

"He-he's supposed to be here," Professor Pembly interjected, her voice shaking as she spoke.

"I see you," he said as he grabbed me by the neck.

The professor pulled at his arms. "Stop!" she cried. "What are you doing?"

My hands covered his wrists, frantically trying to pull them away.

"His family is funding this expedition!" she exclaimed.

With that, he let go of me, and I gasped for air. "Who is your family, boy?"

Who was my family? How the heck was I supposed to know? So I told him the only thing I could—the truth.

"Tobias," I managed.

He raised a brow, but that snarl didn't shift. "Oh? And what manner of work are they in?"

My mind shot all over the place. If I was correct about the time I'd come to based on their clothing, it couldn't be too far from the Titanic days, and Sheena had made me watch that movie. But this was more like Indiana Jones 3. "Shipping," I told him. "The Tobias Lines. And we invest in newspapers, breweries, coal, and property. But my father loves archeology." *Thank you, Sheena, for being so obsessed with this kind of stuff.* I couldn't believe something had rubbed off on me.

The man stepped back. "And your largest ship is?"

"The Amazondotcom," I said matter-of-factly.

"Come with me," he said and stormed away. Professor Pembly and I followed.

He walked at a good pace ahead of us.

Professor Pembly embraced my arm, slowing me down. Her face filled with concern.

"Phillip, you are in danger. He aims to kill you."

CHAPTER 19

LOGAN

My heart raced as the words left her lips. *Kill me?*

Would Aunt Aria let something happen to me? The professor didn't look shocked at all when I said my last name was Tobias. That meant that part was true. So I am a descendant of Phillip. He must have lived or I wouldn't be here. Or he had a sibling and I am a descendant of theirs.

The sun is trying to fry me, the sand is trying to eat me, and now this man, whom no one has introduced is— I didn't get to finish my thought.

There were men waiting under a large tent. "This is Phillip Tobias," the man said gruffly. "He claims to be the son of the Tobias family."

There were a few murmurs of surprise from the men. "The Tobias lineage," one of them said and came closer. I felt like a specimen under a microscope, being examined from all angles.

"Shall we tell him about the temple?" he asked.

The men jeered.

"Right you are! This, my boy, is the key to unlocking the secrets of this temple," he said as he held up an object.

"What secrets?" I asked, afraid to walk closer to see what he had, but knowing that I needed to.

He met my gaze with a sinister grin. "The secrets of the gods, my boy. The power to rule." He set an old wooden chest on a table.

"Open it," he said in a stern voice.

I hesitated for a moment, unsure of what to do. But he grabbed my shoulder, forcibly moving me closer to the chest. " Open it," he repeated.

My hands trembled as I lifted the lid. Inside, there was a small leather-bound book.

"Read it," he ordered.

I opened the first page and recognized the symbols. "The heck I will."

"What?"

"I am not reading this."

"You can not, or you will not?"

"It is in symbols, not letters."

He grabbed me by the nape of my neck and held my head down over the book. The symbols began to glow.

"I told you I could see you. You are a gleamer. The symbols are reacting to you."

They could do whatever they wanted to me. The only way I was going to read what was in that book was if Jesus himself appeared and told me to.

"Did you think we did not see through you?"

I turned. He wasn't talking to me, but to Professor Pembly, whose arms were being held behind her by one of the men. "Where one of you is, others come. This blasted hope you have draws them near."

"Let her go." *Where did that come from?* I was surprised that I said it.

The man grinned. "You will read?"

I nodded, and the man motioned for the other to let the professor go.

"Son of Tobias, owner of The Amazondotcom. You may begin."

I focused on the glowing symbols. They began to transform into letters that I could understand. "Thunder..." I glanced around at them and over at the professor. "Only happens when it's raining..."

The man watched me with intense interest, as he nodded. "Yes," he breathed. "Yes, that's it."

I continued to recite the lyrics from one of the Fleetwood Mac songs Sheena loved so much, and as I spoke, the area grew brighter and a gust of wind blew through the tent. The pages of the journal turned on their own.

Everyone was engrossed in the pages, oblivious to anything else.

Without warning, the professor stepped forward with a lantern and smashed it into the man's head, shattering into pieces. He crumpled to the ground, unconscious. The other men were taken aback for a moment, unsure of what to do before scrambling to react as a wall of flames erupted before us. It was enough time for me to grab the book and Professor Pembly to take my hand and pull me away.

We emerged from the tent. Lightning flashed across the sky. In moments, a sandstorm descended upon the area and pummeled us. Whips of pain crossed my skin. The men shouted in anger behind us, but we couldn't see them.

I shielded my eyes with my arm. The Professor pulled me closer, took a scarf from around her waist and held it to my face. I couldn't see her, but I could feel her guiding me. It was unnerving, feeling everything this Phillip was going through as though I were him, but still myself.

"You have sight, but are blind. You have everything you need."

Who said that?

Bright light expanded in front of me. Even through my closed eyelids, I could see the glow. There was only one light like that, pulsing and radiating power.

"I will guide you."

My guardian angel? No, Phillip's.

As the sandstorm raged on, I stumbled forward, pressing the scarf into my face. The only thing I could see was the faint pulsing light that led us.

The wind howled around us. The sand lashed at the exposed skin of my hands.

Suddenly, I heard a growling noise, and I froze. The professor's grip tightened on my hand. "Don't be afraid," she yelled. "Just keep moving forward."

We walked for what seemed like hours. Finally, the wind died down, and the sand settled around us. We stood in the middle of a vast desert, with nothing but the moon and stars to light our way.

"Are you okay?" asked Professor Pembly, her voice soft and gentle.

"I'm fine," I replied, feeling a sense of calm wash over me. "Thanks to you."

She smiled, and I could feel the warmth of her like an embrace. "Anytime," she said. She tapped the book. "Keep it safe. I'll always be here for you."

"You?" asked Phillip.

Suddenly, I was back in my bedroom. My head was spinning.

"What you experienced was real and true." It was Aunt Aria's voice, but she was nowhere around.

Real? So that really happened to Phillip. He took the book with him. The Lumen. The book that my grandfather left for Sheena.

The professor... She was more than a gleamer. She was a guardian. Phillip's guardian. She had taken human form and saved him from the Murk and its followers. *The key and the book. The key and the book. Wait. What did I really read? I paced the floor. The key. It's not what people think it is.*

"Logan!" Theodore called.

"Is there still time? How long have I been gone?"

"What are you talking about? You just came up here," said Theodore.

"Where is Aunt Aria?"

"With Sheena's mom and the twins. We need to go."

"I'll be down in a second."

Theodore looked at me skeptically and went back downstairs.

My hand covered my mouth. *What just happened?*

"Logan!" Aunt Aria exclaimed and hurried up the hall.

"What I experienced was real and true? How did you do that?"

"First, calm down. This is your first time experiencing my gleam, but I saw it. I saw it all," she whispered and pulled me aside. She looked puzzled. "You experienced more than what Sheena experienced when she went there."

"Wait, what?"

"You went to the exact same time and place that Sheena went to."

"When did she go there?"

"A few days ago."

"Why did you send her there?"

"I didn't. Heaven decides where you go, not me."

"So you never intended to take me back to before the Murk took Sheena?"

"Is that what you were trying to do?"

I nodded. Didn't she see that I just wanted to bring Sheena back?

"Logan, did I tell you that's what I was going to do?"

"No, I just thought—"

"Stop thinking and listen to me."

"Sheena's gleam ended sooner than it should have. Although it had something to do with her... It was about you."

CHAPTER 20

SHEENA

Someone help me! But who? Who would hear me? And if they could, who had the ability to get me out of there, other than God? *The Angelus Bellator? No.* He was too new to all of this. Maybe when he got stronger—*but would I survive that long?* Draven had. But what if the Murk had other plans for me and didn't want me alive?

I prayed inside. Nana always made me memorize bible verses as a kid. I just realized it was for times such as now, when I would need them most. *Be strong and of a good courage, fear not, nor be afraid of them: for the LORD thy God, he it is that doth go with thee; he will not fail thee, nor forsake thee.* I recited it over and over until I drifted away and then heard the verse in my sleep.

"Use your dream," I heard in a whisper. It was faint, but it was there. The voice was familiar.

"Chana? Are you here?"

Her features became clearer with each second. All at once, there she was. Her eyes glimmered as she approached me, a mirror image of the last time I had last seen her. Braids curled at the ends, hanging from beneath a white hat. White coat with faux fur along the hood. "You are dreaming. I'm in your dream."

"But how can you do that? You've never done that before. How can you just enter my dream or unconscious state?"

"Sheena, this is no time for you to try to understand the mechanics of it all. It is the only way I can reach you. And stop talking before you mumble something out loud. Take comfort in knowing He hears your prayers even now."

"He, meaning?" I pointed up at the sky.

"Yes, stop talking."

"When you prayed, your faith strengthened you enough for me to do this. Your unwavering hope is as much a blessing as it is a curse. A blessing because it is what may save you. A curse because of those who seek to destroy it." That wasn't Chana's teen voice, but her angel warrior voice.

I started to speak, but stopped. I wanted to hang on to this moment as long as I could. Being near her, even though it was only in a dream, brought me hope that I would be freed soon.

"The Murk thinks that it has figured out the mystery of it all. But it has not. Neither have you. There is still time, and there is still a way out. Keep praying, don't lose heart. When you next close your eyes, I will be there with an update."

In the dream, sweat began pouring from my head. Intense heat hugged every inch of my body. *I'm waking.* I coughed uncontrollably. Chana faded, and so did my surroundings.

"Please hold on. We are coming for you," were the last words I heard before my eyes shot open. What I saw wasn't the Murk but the wooden beams of a ceiling.

I gasped for air and looked down at the sweat drenching my clothes. The dream had been so vivid, so real. Chana's voice still echoed in my mind, urging me to hold on, to keep praying.

My hands glided across the dimpled patchwork quilt beneath me. I got up from the bed, my bare feet cold against the hardwood floor. The dim light above me flickered, casting shadows that danced across the weathered wood walls, the paint peeling and chipping in some places, illuminating dust particles in the air.

My body felt heavy and sluggish, like it was made of lead.

As I walked to the window of the cabin, I saw a figure in the distance standing at the edge of the woods. It was too dark to make out any features.

My heart raced as I opened the window, letting in a gust of chilly wind. I leaned out and shouted, "Who are you? What do you want?"

The figure remained silent.

"Answer me!" I yelled, feeling a mix of fear and anger.

Suddenly, the figure stepped forward, revealing himself in the moonlight. In seconds, the door to the room creaked open. My heart pounded hard in my chest as I turned toward the door and stepped backward against the windowsill. The man was dressed in dark robes, his face obscured by a hood.

"Who are you?" I demanded.

"I think you know, Sheena Meyer."

It's him. Calm yourself, Sheena. My thoughts knew what I needed to do, but my brain wasn't listening. *Don't be afraid. Stop giving it what it wants. Stop strengthening it.*

He waited.

"If you want me to cry or scream, I'm not going to." I looked toward the fireplace on the opposite side of the bed. "And why all the illusions? Surely I'm not in a cabin in what I assume is upper Michigan. What, Mackinac Island? And I'm supposed to be camping or something? That isn't what I'm here for, right? But that's probably what you're about to say next. 'Camping is not what you are here for, Sheena Meyer,'" I said, lowering my voice. "What else have you got? Your usual routine isn't cutting it anymore."

Who in the world did I think I was? I told myself to stop talking, but once again, the message didn't get from my brain to my mouth.

Drake stepped closer, and he carefully pushed the hood back away from his face.

I gasped. "You're not Drake."

"No, I'm not."

Why does he look so familiar? His pupils were the deepest black, and they bore into mine with an intensity that made my knees weak. The man didn't move. He just stood there, watching me with those dark eyes. "My name is Marcus," he said, his voice low and smooth. His face was chiseled and angular, with high cheekbones and a sharp jawline. "And you, Sheena Meyer, are going to help me."

"Help you?" I asked.

Marcus wore a cold, cruel grin—one that held a strange familiarity, as though I had encountered him in a dream. "Help me take down the gleamers."

"What? That's not going to happen."

"I see you're not easily intimidated," the man said, his voice low and menacing. "But you should be. You're in grave danger, Sheena Meyer. And only I can protect you."

I eyed him skeptically. "Protect me from what?"

His hands stretched out to the sides, palms up. The walls of the cabin disappeared and what was left was the churning Murk around us.

For the moment, the Murk's fire and fumes weren't choking me. And though I had seen the inside of the Murk already—spent hours inside of it—seeing it writhing and surrounding me was no less frightening.

Ever since I was a kid, I had a habit of laughing when I shouldn't. Especially when I was nervous. So that's what I did. It began as a nervous chuckle and then a full-blown guffaw. Marcus only watched.

"I'm sorry, I think I'm having too much fun with this foolishness. Give me a second to calm down."

"You're right, Sheena Meyer. Fun is not what you're here for." His voice seemed to come from all around me, as if being played through an amplifier. "But perhaps, entertainment is."

Before I could respond, he lunged at me, his hands reaching for my neck. I pushed at him, but he was too strong. His fingers tightened around my throat.

My eyes widened, looking into his. I did recognize him. He was the same man from the archeological site that Aunt Aria's gleam showed me. How was he here?

I gasped for air, struggling to break free from his clutch. Each breath felt like fire in my lungs, and I knew that if I didn't do something fast, I would black out.

From the corner of my eye, I saw arms reaching out of the Murk. *There's another one?* They reached around Marcus and snatched him backward, throwing him inside the Murk. Then the person stepped out of it.

"Sheena, are you okay?"

"Draven?"

CHAPTER 21

LOGAN

The lack of sleep is messing with my mind. It had to be, because Aunt Aria told me the gleam/time travel, or whatever I just experienced, was about me. How could Sheena's gleam have been about me? I searched Aunt Aria's eyes for answers, but all I found was a puzzled gaze that left me with more questions than before. "Did that really just happen?"

Aunt Aria looked irritated and possibly about to slap me to knock some sense into me.

"Okay, it happened, but now it seems like a dream."

"Logan, the gleam is a mysterious gift bestowed upon us by Heaven itself. It doesn't always do what we expect or want it to do. It has its own purpose and plan."

Her words only frustrated me further. I clenched the journal. I had always believed that the gleam was a tool to help us set things right, to fix the wrongdoings of the Murk. But if Aunt Aria was correct in that we didn't control the gleam, what hope did we have in saving Sheena?

"Then what am I supposed to do now—with the things I was shown—experienced?" I asked, my voice barely above a whisper.

"You're a smart boy. I'm sure you'll figure it out," Aunt Aria stated, the gleam in her eyes expanding in and out like the beat of a heart.

She turned to go back down the hall, took a couple of steps, and came back. "The journey is all I'm supposed to help with. If I were you, I would go downstairs and have a talk with the descendants of the City of Gleamers."

"And say what?"

"Really? You have no questions about what you saw?"

"Oh, I do."

"Ask *them*."

Aunt Aria continued down the hall. I descended the stairs at a slow, steady pace and watched and listened from the landing to all the conversations coming from the living room and down the hall.

My countenance perked up for a moment, seeing Ariel walk toward me to go up the stairs carrying a tray. "Is that for the twins?"

"Yes, they are so dehydrated."

"Any additional news from them?"

"Not yet, but they are getting stronger."

"Where are the Knights?" I already knew, but I asked anyway, to keep the conversation going, if only for a moment.

"In the basement with Corey. He has a plan."

"Okay, I'll head down there shortly."

I gave Ariel the best grin I could, considering everything, and she did the same, allowing her hand to brush mine as she passed. Her healer gleamer scent lingered as she carefully climbed the stairs with the tray. A few steps up, she looked back, knowing I was still there and watching her. With a subtle nod, she gestured toward the living room. "Go ahead." Her bright eyes held mine a moment before breaking away.

I nodded. Ariel always knew things. Her subtle prod was just what I needed to get me off that landing. I walked right into the center of the adults in the living room and stood next to the coffee table. No one paid much attention to me, so I cleared my throat loudly. "If you are not a descendant of the City of Gleamers, I need you to leave the room."

All heads turned to me, each face with a different expression. Some looked confused, others suspicious, and a few downright hostile, because I was a kid telling them what to do. I held my ground, trying my best to exude confidence, even though my heart was beating a mile a minute.

Several people stood and made their way past me, through the dining room entrance. Only a handful remained seated, watching me intently.

This was it, the moment of truth.

"Those that remain here are descendants of the City of Gleamers," said Nana. "Speak freely, son."

"That's right, we've got you," said Ma, Justin's grandmother.

Mr. Knight, Ariel's father, nodded toward me and I nodded back.

"I've seen something," I began, my voice faltering slightly. "Something that I can't explain. It was like a dream, but I know it was real. And Aunt Aria told me to come to you for answers."

They shared a knowing glance before one of them spoke up. "What did you see?"

Instead of telling them the whole vision, or journey, as Aunt Aria called it. I told them about the man who wanted me to read from the book.

"The Lumen?" asked Nana.

"Yes."

Stephen Woodruff walked into the room. I recognized him from the back cover of his novels. "I heard there's a meeting going on in here that I'm supposed to be a part of."

He leaned against the doorway holding a cane and listened to my story. "Ah... Aria has quite a gleam. There aren't many travelers anymore. What you experienced was real and true."

"So I've heard."

"Did you see the owl too?" he asked excitedly.

Really? Was that all he wanted to know? "Yes, I did."

He smirked. "Angels unaware."

He was beginning to irritate me, and no one else was saying anything, so I had to deal with him. "What's that supposed to mean?"

"Angels are always with you, son. You didn't go there alone. Aria has the gift, but angels take you."

It made sense, but we weren't getting anywhere, so I got straight to the point. "From what I understand, you are a big historian, especially when it comes to gleamers. What do you know about an archeological site, Phillip, a man wearing a turban, and the Lumen?"

Mr. Woodruff's face turned serious as he slowly walked towards me. "I know more than I care to admit," he said in a grave tone. "The Lumen held great power."

Logan noticed he referenced the Lumen in the past tense. *So he knows Ariel threw it in that chest, destroying it.* "You mean the words in it?"

"Words hold power, and the Lumen had been sought after for centuries by those who wished to wield that power for their own gain. What do you know of what you saw?"

I hesitated for a moment before answering. "Phillip was at an archaeological site, and he was holding the Lumen. And there was a man wearing a turban who was going to kill him if he didn't read from it."

Mr. Woodruff's eyes widened in surprise. "You saw all of that? You may have stumbled upon something big, son. Something that's been hidden for centuries." He straightened and tapped his cane on the ground. "Come." He motioned for me to follow him into the dining room. We all did. Nana closed the door that led into the butler's pantry.

Mr. Woodruff took a briefcase from the floor and placed it on the dining room table. The case had a three-digit tumbler lock on each side. He put in the combinations, pulled on the locks, and the latches opened. I don't know what I expected to see when he opened the briefcase, but after the top rose, I realized I'd been holding my breath. He sifted through the case, tossed several journals onto the table, and pulled out a thick leather-bound book. "This is the history I've documented." He flipped through the book until he found what he was looking for and then pointed at a grainy black-and-white photo. "Is this the archaeological site you saw?"

"Yes, that's it!" It was eerie seeing it, and Professor Pembly, again. I could hardly believe I had been there.

"It was discovered in the early 1900s by a team of British archaeologists. They found a lot of strange artifacts there.

"As I understand it, the man wearing the turban was once one of the guardians of the Lumen. They were sworn to protect the book at all costs, and they would stop at nothing to ensure its safety."

"He wasn't a gleamer. But he knew Phillip was."

Mr. Woodruff nodded. "He was last known as Marcus." He looked up at me and noticed the surprise in my eyes.

"Tell him," said Ma.

Mr. Woodruff nodded, but hesitated.

"What? Tell me what?"

"Marcus embodied the Murk."

CHAPTER 22

SHEENA

Draven saved me. Not Drake, but Draven. Somehow, he was himself again. Instantly, we were transported from the smoldering, writhing lava to a room in a house. His house. I looked out the window and recognized the yard. His bedroom, maybe?

"Sheena, are you okay?" He stared at me, his eyes softening. "You can trust me, Sheena. I'm not here to hurt you."

"Yes, I'm okay," I managed to say, though my voice was weak. "But where did you come from, and why did you help me?"

Draven's eyes narrowed, his expression a mix of concern and determination. "I've been studying the Murk for years, and I know its ways. I couldn't let you face it alone." He looked away for a moment, a strange expression on his face. Then he met my eyes again and nodded. "Yes, Sheena. I saw you were in danger, and I had to act."

"But how?"

"It weakens. That's when I'm able to fight it off." He looked away again. "But it still has a hold on me."

I shook my head. "Please, Draven. I understand you've been here a long time. I need to know how to survive this."

Draven sighed, his eyes scanning the room around us. The whole scene wavered, flickering like a candle in a draft. "The Murk is not what it seems. It's a trap designed for those foolish enough to believe they can conquer it."

"I don't understand, but I think we can destroy it."

He shook his head. "While I can, I need to thank you, Sheena. For everything. I could hear you. Those words of love weaken and anger the Murk." He looked away. "For once, I don't feel so alone in this torment. I'm sorry I brought you here."

"You didn't. I chose it. And you weren't alone. Your sisters were here too."

"They... They're not like me."

I didn't understand what he was getting at, and he didn't say anything further, so I asked what I really wanted to know—afraid that if I stopped talking, he would disappear. "Why did you free me from him?"

"I didn't know what he was going to do to you. But also...so you can free *me*."

He believes that I can, even now? "Why can't you do it yourself?"

The room around us began to dissolve and reform like a constantly changing video game. Whatever controlled this illusion was breaking down.

Draven held a finger to his lips and looked up at the ceiling. "We don't have much time. We need to weaken it more. It's the only way." He stepped forward and kissed me.

It wasn't just a brief kiss on the lips; it held a deeper significance. Within that shared moment, there was something unmistakable. Love.

He looked into my eyes and released me. "You've read my journal. I know you have, because it's gone. Remember what's in it," he said, backing away.

"Wait, who was that man?"

"He is not a man."

There were more pieces to this puzzle than I ever imagined. So many layers. It was naïve of us to think that what we saw was all there was. That's what Nana tried to show me when she talked about knowing everything about a situation before forming opinions. We knew nothing and walked into this blindly.

I called out to Draven, but he didn't answer.

The worst thing the Murk could do was leave me alone with thoughts entering and leaving me like the on and off ramps of a freeway. The moment with Draven was better than the silence. Being alone, lifeless, was horrible. I'd rather hear the Murk's creepy voice. Then, at least I would know I was alive. Or was I?

At that thought, a jolt of pain passed through me that took my breath away. The Murk came at me with a vengeance. The torment was so great, I felt myself passing out.

I awakened hearing the Murk's roar. Its smokey presence became disjointed, revealing parts of the real world on the outside. Suddenly everything went black, and then I was in another place—observing the world from a higher perspective.

Is this the place between heaven and hell?

"I don't belong here." I looked up and saw nothing but the bright, pale blue sky. Below me was darkness. "I am a stranger in a strange land." I had no idea what I was saying. My vision was blurred, and my ears filled with the sound of rushing wind.

"Sheena..."

"Chana?"

"Good, you are asleep."

"No, I'm not. I passed out."

"Yes, but I did not want to say that."

"Are they close to saving me? I don't know how much longer I can endure the pain. It's much worse now. And I finally talked to Draven. And there is someone else here, and he is pure evil."

"Corey has a plan. So do the guardians. We will fight for the Knights in the spiritual realm."

"But what about the man, Marcus?"

"He is who Principal Vernon would have become."

I remembered our middle school principal and how I considered him a father figure until I found he was really evil and helping the Murk.

"Stay away from him. He revealed himself to you. That is not good."

"Are you telling me we thought Drake was our problem, but all the while, this guy was?"

"That is exactly what I am saying."

"I saw him at the archeological site before you pulled me away. Even then, he tried to kill me."

"Not exactly."

"What do you mean?"

"I acted prematurely. You did not see everything that happened with Phillip."

"Chana, I don't understand."

"And you are not going to," she replied. Her voice drifting further away.

"What did you say? I can't hear you anymore."

"Stop talking," she screamed. "You are waking!"

CHAPTER 23

THEODORE

The hours were all blending together. Each of the Knights knew their part in Corey's plan. Time would tell if it would work. But first, we had to get to Phoenix. Still, no one had heard from Cameron or Quincy, and we feared we had waited so long that there was no telling what we would find when we arrived. Cameron's rage may have caused him to see red and forget who he was, or *whose* he was.

We had a covenant with angels—with heaven. Not a contract between people, but a covenant with God. I wiped my hand across my face. I was one to talk. I had been bumping heads with Logan like crazy. Maybe we all needed a reminder of who we were.

As we walked out of Sheena's house and over to Nana's car, I couldn't shake the feeling that we were being watched. Every time I turned around, shadows flitted about, but when I looked closer, there was no one there. I glanced up at the windows of the house, but didn't see curtains moving or anything, and got in the car beside Chana.

Chana shifted in her seat. Her eyes darted around, taking in the surroundings, as if she, too, felt a sense of unease.

"You okay?" I asked.

"Yeah, it's just an eerie day."

"You got that right."

After a few minutes of driving in silence, Parker suddenly said, "We gotta find someone who knows what that key Logan has opens. These clues and secrets are like hidden thorns. How did Sheena survive like this?"

"I don't know, but I don't want this for her."

"But it's our lives, too, now. When we were knighted, it was like saying, 'Yeah I'm down for whatever, bring it on.' We accepted it, bro," said Parker.

That realization brought on more silence.

It was the middle of the day. We pulled up to the one-story ranch-style home and parked. Sheena would have called it a farmhouse style, mid century modern, or some other style I didn't know. I only knew that it was a long house with a three-car garage. A white Tesla was parked in the driveway.

"Is this it?" asked Parker.

"Yep, that's Phoenix's car."

Chana pointed in front of the next house. "Corey, is that your car?"

He was in the front passenger seat. "Yeah, that's it."

"Why is it still here?" I asked. After so much time had passed, I didn't expect it to be there.

"I don't know, but it looks peaceful enough out here," said Logan. "Maybe Cameron didn't do anything to Phoenix."

"Maybe he's been gathering information, or the Murk came here and they're injured in there. Maybe they've been arrested," said Parker.

Chana reached around me and punched his chest with the side of her fist.

"What? I didn't say it happened. I said *Maybe*."

"*Maybe* you can get out of the car."

Corey opened the car door and looked behind us as Justin ran up from his truck. He had followed us over. "Yo, run down to the car and see if it's empty," Corey instructed.

Justin nodded, ran down to the car, looked inside the driver's side and back seat windows and jogged back. "No one's in there."

"Let's go then. This way," Corey instructed. We headed toward the side of the house.

Parker stood at the front door, pointing at it. "Aren't we going to ring the—"

"Just come on," I told him.

Corey motioned toward the windows. "Logan, which bedroom is Phoenix's?"

Logan pointed.

"Why do you know that? You've been here before?" I asked.

"You don't know my every move. It's none of your business. Plus, he's not a threat anymore. He's one of us. And I'm getting tired of talking about this and having to defend myself to you."

"You're not helping, Theodore," Chana whispered to me.

"Whatever," I replied, eyeing Logan.

Along the side of the house, past a concrete slab with a table and four metal chair frames without cushions, was a small courtyard.

"Oh, shoot." I pointed at the sliding doors across from it. One was wide open.

"We're going in," said Corey.

We walked carefully up to the house as if the sound of our footsteps would set off an alarm.

"Please, please, please," said Corey.

"Please what?" asked Justin.

"Just praying Cameron didn't do something stupid."

There were no curtains or blinds covering the doors. Corey poked his head inside and then walked in. We followed and then stood there and waited, listening for any sounds. It was a sitting room, nothing out of the ordinary. Then we heard voices and hurried around the corner, following the light pouring into the hall.

It looked like a tornado had come inside and only attacked the one room of the house. Quincy sat on the top of the back of a chair with her feet on the seat, her elbows on her knees, and her hands clasped together, looking toward the back of the long room.

"Dang, Cameron. What the heck, dude?" I asked.

"I let him in my house, and this is what he did to it," said Phoenix.

"And Quincy?"

She held up her hands, innocently. "I've stayed out of the way, watching it all go down. I came to make sure Cameron didn't do anything that Sheena wouldn't agree with."

"You? You're thinking rationally for once? I don't believe it," said Parker.

"It's true," said Phoenix. "She spent most of the time holding him back."

"James 2: *Mercy triumphs over judgement*," said Cameron.

Corey shook his head. "I don't think that's the context that scripture was meant for."

"So what's happening now?" I asked. "You've been gone for hours."

Quincy picked up half a sandwich from the desk behind her and bit into it. "Zero-sum game."

"That's exactly why I didn't bash his head in," said Cameron. "It wouldn't really benefit anything."

"Did you try?" I whispered. "I mean, he has you by a good three inches and twenty pounds."

Quincy spoke with her mouth full. "Yeah, he tried. A lot of good that did."

"You made a sandwich?" asked Parker.

I stepped further into the room. "So what's the answer to the big question? You've been here long enough to find out," I told Cameron.

Cameron only lifted a hand toward Phoenix, so I turned to him. "Why weren't you with us last night?"

"That wasn't last night. It was this morning."

"Last night, this morning, whatever. You know what I mean. We needed you. Sheena needed you. She needed the Knights of the Gleam. That's why we were knighted, to fight this thing, and you ghosted us." My voice was rising, but I tried to stay calm, fighting the urge to lunge at him. What would it solve? Plus, what Quincy had said struck a nerve. I didn't want to do anything Sheena wouldn't agree with. Well, unless he tested me.

Phoenix placed a hand on his hip and rubbed under his nose. "I couldn't."

"Wait, where are you parents? Why haven't they rushed in here with the Police or something?"

"We already covered that," said Quincy, picking at her teeth. "They're not home."

"Phoenix, I think you're not being there, hurt us. It was supposed to be all of us, like all the disciples or something," said Logan.

Phoenix sighed. "I don't know what to say except that I'm sorry. And I've been saying it repeatedly for hours. I haven't been to sleep just like you—"

"And you weren't there because?"

Phoenix's head dropped. "Because I was afraid."

He sat on the box spring, since the mattress was flipped off the bed. "I didn't want to hear from you. I didn't want to see any of you—see the disappointment in your eyes. None of you know what it's like. To be a part of that thing and then be free of it. The thought of going back in there—"

We were silent. A part of me felt badly for him, but a larger part didn't. "So to save yourself, you let the Murk take Sheena?"

"Exactly what I said," Cameron retorted.

"That wasn't what I wanted—never what I wanted. I didn't even know it happened until Cameron came here. I wouldn't have let her go there in the first place."

"Me either," I replied. "I mean, I shouldn't have."

"You running from your purpose only made things worse," said Corey.

"I know...But I-I'm here now. What can I do?"

"Help us get her back. We have 24 hours—"

"Had 24 hours," I reminded him. "We have about 13 now."

"After that, we've lost Sheena, and the Murk will be the most powerful it's ever been. She contains all the power it needs," said Logan.

"What have you been doing here all this time?" I asked, looking from Phoenix, to Cameron, to Quincy.

Quincy shrugged and hopped off the chair. "Once they realized fighting was getting them nowhere, Cameron decided to get all the information he could out of him."

I rolled my fingers around each other. "Like?"

"Like what he knows about the Murk's weaknesses," Cameron spoke up. "And where the Murk has taken Sheena. We've been tracking down any leads we can find, meaning Murked-out kids, thinking they could lead us to that creature from hell."

"But there's something you guys haven't thought about," Quincy interjected, still picking at her teeth.

Logan and Corey moved closer to her at the same time as me. "What do you mean by that?"

"Doesn't Sheena have her phone?"

"Of course she does." When were Chana and Sheena ever without their phones? They texted each other even when they were right next to each other.

"Then we've got her," said Quincy.

"Oh, I know where she's going with this," said Chana, speaking for the first time since we entered the house. "Mrs. Meyer installed that *find my teen app* on her phone."

"No trust there," said Parker.

"As if Sheena didn't give her a reason? Boy, be quiet."

"No," said Logan, as if he were thinking aloud. "It's more like she was preparing for what she knew might come to pass."

Parker frowned. "Come to pass? Why is he sounding all biblical?"

For the first time that day, I think the heaviness among us lifted.

"Okay," said Corey, hitting his fist into his hand. "We have an idea on how to find her. What else did you talk about before we got here? Did you come up with plan?"

"Sort of..." Cameron replied.

"But you already have a plan," I reminded him.

"No, I want to hear this," said Corey.

"We talked about how to find the Murk's weak spots," said Cameron. "So we can get inside of it..."

"Are you serious?" I asked. "Is that possible?"

Cameron nodded. "That's what we've planned to do—get inside of it and bring back Sheena."

I choked on my saliva. "What?" I tried to say, but coughed.

"What in tarnation?" asked Justin. I pointed at him, nodding, telling them that's what I meant.

"I don't know, guys. That sounds like a suicide mission," said Parker.

"We're running out of options," Quincy told him. "We've got to get inside and save her."

"Quincy, it's not that simple," I said. "And you're not even a Knight."

Cameron moved closer to me. "Listen, I know you're afraid of what could happen. But you owe it to Sheena to do everything in your power to save her."

I looked away, blinking back tears. Sheena had always been the bravest of us all, diving headfirst into danger without a second thought. She would have done anything to protect us. And now it was our turn to return the favor.

"Okay," I said, wiping my eyes. "What do you need me to do, because the way you just came at me, I assume this is about me."

Cameron grinned and lifted a hand, which I clasped. "We need you to go undercover."

My heart raced as I tried to comprehend what he meant. "Undercover? As in... infiltrating the Murk?"

Cameron nodded, his eyes sparkling. "That's right. You and Bradly."

"Oh, me and Bradly. Like that's okay?"

"It has to be you two. You've been infected by it already. We can fool it."

"We're not the only ones. There's one more person..." I replied.

I turned to her, and so did everyone else.

"Me?" asked Quincy.

"Don't worry, you will be okay," said Cameron. "If anyone can do this, Quinn, you can."

"No doubt," said Corey, in agreement.

I shook my head. "Don't tell her that. You can't promise her that."

"You just said, 'we've got to get inside and save her,'" Parker told Quincy.

"Yes, but I meant helping to get the gleamers inside who can shoot bolts of energy through their hands."

"Cameron, how do you think this will work?" I asked.

"Ever heard of the Trojan horse?"

"I know you're not talking about that huge, hollow wooden horse the Greeks used to get inside enemy lines during the Trojan War," said Justin.

"That's the one."

"You do know that's supposedly a myth, right?" asked Quincy.

I stared at Cameron, starting to understand what he was saying, but concerned nonetheless.

Parker walked around the room until he was in full view of everyone. "Does no one else find this ludicrous?"

Corey suddenly looked up. "Oh snap. I get what he's saying. They're the Trojan horse."

"Really? It took you that long?" asked Cameron.

"But we can't fit anything inside of them," said Parker.

Justin smacked him on the back of the head. "They already have what they need inside of them. Well, maybe not Quincy."

"Didn't Sheena tell you? I'm a gleamer too."

"Stop playing."

"No, seriously."

Everyone hushed and turned to her.

"Will y'all stop staring at me? Sheesh. I was lying."

I pointed at her. "See, that kind of stuff can get you in trouble. This is no time for games."

"I could be a gleamer," she mumbled.

Logan said something, and I turned to him. His eyes were focused on the ground.

"What did you say?" I asked.

This time, he looked up and directly at Phoenix. "It won't work unless you are leading them."

"What part?" I asked.

"Any of it."

Phoenix shook his head.

Logan remained fixed on Phoenix, unwavering.

Phoenix shifted uncomfortably, avoiding eye contact with anyone in the room.

"You don't understand," said Logan. "I'm not asking."

I had never seen Logan like this before. His calm demeanor was gone, and I was unsure of what was going to happen next. The slightest spark emanated from his hands and wrapped around his fingers before disappearing.

Corey held his hands up. "Wait a minute, wait a minute. How are you trying to say this Trojan horse will fool the Murk?"

Cameron sighed. "The darkness will have to enter them again."

We all talked at the same time.

"Only a little," said Cameron. "You have to be strong enough to handle it, and I think you are."

"That's because it's not you who has to do it. You have no idea what it's like," I told him.

Cameron put his hands up. "Do we want to save Sheena or not?"

I nodded. "Of course we do."

"Hidden thorns," Parker mumbled.

"What do you mean by that?" asked Cameron.

"He said that in the car, too."

"I'm talking about all the potential risks of what we are about to do—things that we have no idea are waiting for us."

"Project Hidden Thorns it is then," Cameron said. He lifted his fist out in front of him.

I knocked it down. "That's not for you to do. What do you say, Logan?"

He looked up at me, surprised. Then he nodded and lifted his fist. The rest of us placed our hands on top of his. Except for Phoenix. He stood at a distance, leaning against the wall with hands in the pockets of his sweatpants. His triceps tensed and bulged from under his T-shirt, his hair hung down to his chest, shielding his face from view. He shook his head, turned his back to us, and covered his face.

We waited. This couldn't go down without him. We needed him. But it was his decision to make. If he chose not to help, we would have to keep Logan from zapping him and figure out a way without him. There is always a Plan B.

Finally, Phoenix turned back, red faced. He slowly approached and laid his hand on top of ours.

CHAPTER 24

THEODORE

"Now that that's over, here," said Cameron. He tossed a phone at Phoenix.

"You confiscated his phone?" asked Parker.

I picked it up first. "Is this yours?" I asked, pointing it at Phoenix.

"Yeah."

"What's the passcode?" I asked.

"None of your business." Phoenix reached for it, but I swung it out of the way.

"I thought we were cool now, Bro. What's up? You got something to hide? What's the passcode?"

Phoenix studied me for a moment. "Hold it still," he instructed, tapping on the phone screen.

I eyed him closely, searching for any sign of nervousness, but found none. The screen unlocked and I glanced over at Logan. As far as I was concerned, we were cool now. He had redeemed himself. Especially after being ready to make Phoenix help us by force if need be. There was no better way to show his loyalty and how far he would go to help Sheena.

Still, I was curious about what he and Logan had been texting—if they were—even if it was harmless. This was the part of me that bugged Sheena the most. I wouldn't let things go.

"What's up, Theodore," asked Cameron.

"Nothing," just looking.

For some reason, I went to his photos first and scrolled through them, back as far as they went. Then, I slowly scrolled forward and stopped. I couldn't believe my eyes. "What's this?"

"What?" the Knights asked as they approached.

I held the phone up and showed it to Phoenix.

"Why are you in my photos?" he asked.

"Just answer the question."

"That's from a bootcamp."

"What kind of bootcamp," asked Corey.

"For troubled teenagers."

"Chana, look," I said, pulling her closer.

She squinted at the phone. "Is that—"

I nodded.

"What?" asked Phoenix.

"The twins. Those are the twins with you."

"What twins? Wait, you mean the twins that are at Sheena's house?" asked Cameron.

"Hold on," Phoenix said with his hand up, looking as if he were about to sprint out of the room. His eyes grew wide. I guess Cameron hadn't filled him in on that yet. He tapped his fist on his forehead. "What are their names? Ugh, why can't I remember? Hues. Tiffany. Tiffany and Alexis. I know you're not saying they're at Sheena's house right now?"

"Yeah, why? Sheena saved them. She pulled them out of the Murk. You would know that if you were there," I replied.

Phoenix raised a brow. "Are you sure?"

"We all saw it. Why?" asked Quincy.

"Those girls are evil," said Phoenix.

"Yeah, we know. They were part of the Murk."

"No, they were evil before that. Look at that photo again. Do I look happy?"

"No. You kind of look like them," said Parker.

"That was no regular bootcamp. Our parents may have thought it was a military-style intervention to "fix" their unruly teenage delinquent and turn them into a law-abiding member of society. But in reality, it was one of the Murk camps."

"One of the Murk camps?" asked Quincy.

"Of course," said Cameron, snapping his fingers. "When we helped Sheena save those kids that were kidnapped and being kept in that warehouse, remember they were going to be shipped off to farms where they were being brainwashed and programmed. The feds busted all of those farms. We should've known the Murk had another way of getting to kids. Think about it. Most of them were already troublemakers, so it wouldn't be too hard for the Murk to not only get stronger from them, but to finish them off to where they no longer know who they are."

I handed the phone to Phoenix. "They were there because of their brother, Draven, right?"

Phoenix looked confused. "Who is Draven?"

"Cameron, have you told him nothing?"

Cameron shook his head. "I didn't know if he could be trusted yet."

"Logan?"

"I haven't given details about anything," said Logan. "Like you, I wasn't certain about what we were dealing with here."

"Wow, trust much?" asked Phoenix.

"I respect that," I told Logan and motioned to Phoenix. "How would you expect us to trust you after you didn't show up for Sheena at the trailer park?"

"Take it down a notch, Theodore. Look," Corey told Phoenix. "Draven is Drake."

"What do you mean?" asked Phoenix.

"Draven is his real name."

"As in, he's a real person?" Phoenix grimaced and held his head. "He is a real person," he said with his eyes closed. "I'm trying to remember…I'm having glimpses of him, but not enough. Ugh, I wish I could remember more."

"Why can't he remember?" asked Quincy.

"Most of his memories of what he has been through are gone," said Logan.

"That's not a bad thing," she replied, and I realized there were things she probably wanted to forget but couldn't.

"We've been to their house—Draven and the twins," said Justin. "Sheena found a hidden room with an altar in it. The twins were into some dark stuff—"

"With the Murk," Phoenix finished.

"By the way, the caretaker is dead," I told Cameron.

"You're kidding."

"You've missed a lot."

"Was it Drake?"

"I don't think so," said Logan. "Phoenix, do you remember him being with the twins?"

"He wasn't at the camp."

"That's because they actually led the Murk to him," I shared.

Cameron looked shocked. "Why? How?"

"Had you not disappeared, you would've heard all of this."

"Theodore…" Corey said and shook his head.

"Power," said Logan.

"Power for what?" asked Cameron.

"To do what they want and not have to answer to anyone."

"Answer to whom? Their parents? Who else is stopping them from doing what they want?" asked Cameron.

"I don't know, but the Murk used them to get to Draven, better known as Drake."

Phoenix appeared lost in thought for a moment. His brow furrowed and eyes narrowed. He spoke slowly. "You don't have to believe me, but Sheena rescued the wrong ones. It should've been their brother instead of them."

Chana and I exchanged a glance. Quincy walked over and stood on top of one of the mattresses.

"But they seem—" said Cameron.

Phoenix shook his head. "Trust me, those girls are not okay."

"They're so frail," I added, picturing the twins.

"I'm telling you, it's worse than you could ever imagine."

Outside, the wind howled. And with each revelation, the wind found its way inside Phoenix's bedroom, wrapping around me with an icy embrace.

I patted my pockets, wondering where I had set my phone. "Somebody call Mr. Meyer. Hurry!"

"We need to get back to the house," said Corey. "And you're coming with us."

"Let me ask you something," said Phoenix. "Why did you think it was going to let go of its greatest avatar so easily, and why do you think it's Drake?

I was confused. "Greatest? Why would you say greatest? How do you know that? And if not Drake, who? Tell us what you know."

TIME REMAINING: 11 HOURS

CHAPTER 25
BRADLY

There were just too many people in the house for my liking. I carefully stepped down the stairs and around the pool table with several bowls and bottled water on a tray. The Knights who didn't leave with Corey were there in the basement, although Ariel and Seren kept going upstairs, checking on the twins. They said the girls were sleeping peacefully in Sheena's grandmother's bedroom.

"I've got Goulash," I exclaimed. "Sheena's grandmother is up there cooking like a madwoman. You should see the size of the pot this came from. It's like a restaurant would have or something.

"Uh, hello? Jasmine? Bodhi? What's going on down here? You guys are way too quiet."

"Huh?" said Jasmine, sliding a headphone away from her ear.

"I said, 'You guys are too quiet."

"We're focused."

"Well, I brought you food. I've been slaving away in the kitchen. Here you go, Bodhi."

"Thanks," he replied, taking the bowl and sitting it on the table in front of the sofa. "Did you really cook?"

"No, Nana made it. Justin's grandmother is up there helping her. She is off the chain. She's driving everybody nuts, but she can cook. I guess that's where Justin gets it from."

They both tapped away on laptops, but Jasmine also had books open on the floor around her. One of them she held open with her foot and another under her bent knee.

I set the tray down and stepped closer to take a look at what they were working on. "Anything worth mentioning?" I asked.

"Just some basic information at first, but now it's getting interesting," Jasmine replied, not looking up from her screen.

I pulled my braids back so they wouldn't fall into her face as I looked over her at the computer screen. *The city of Muskegon and the fires that burned it down*, I read.

"There's so much information to cover in so little time," said Jasmine. "I know there's something we're missing here, and I'm going to find it."

"Not before I do," said Bodhi.

They both grinned, but didn't look away from their screens.

I settled on the other end of the sofa with a bowl and scooped up a spoonful of goulash. It was warm, and the tomato aroma was comforting, but I couldn't fully appreciate it. The savory spices were overshadowed by the bitter taste of frustration. It really bothered me that I couldn't figure out a way to be helpful. I felt left out, and fiddled with the spoon sulking like an uninvited guest made to sit at the children's table for dinner, instead of with the adults. *Maybe I should have gone with Chana and the boys.* I would have, but Chana had asked that I help with Dingy. But now his mother was with him and he slept in the family room amongst all the chattering up there.

I sat in silence, watching Jasmine and Bodhi work tirelessly to find a solution for setting Sheena free. They were so focused on their work that they didn't even notice me staring at them.

My thoughts drifted to the time Chana and I showed up for Sheena, crashing Chana's father's truck through the warehouse, just as Logan's father was about to kill Sheena. We saved her. And as scared as I was, it felt good to help.

I set my bowl on the coffee table and knelt beside Jasmine. "What can I do?"

She and Bodhi looked surprised, but quickly welcomed me in. Jasmine handed me a stack of books. "Sort through these pages at the places where I've placed the sticky notes and write down what I've highlighted. Let me know if anything catches your attention."

"Meaning?"

"If something doesn't make sense, there may be a reason for that. You may catch something I didn't."

"Well, I'd better get to work then." I slid into one of the worn leather chairs, behind Jasmine and Bodhi, at the table near the pool table, and flipped through the stack of books that Jasmine had handed me. The pages were filled with her meticulous notes and colorful sticky tabs, marking important sections and highlighting key points. Sheena was going to have a fit when she saw how her books were marked up.

After about an hour had passed, I closed the book I worked through and flipped it over in my hand. Jasmine and Bodhi wore headphones, so I wasn't sure if they would hear me.

"Hey," we all said at the same time.

They looked over at each other and I watched them each push a headphone back from one of their ears.

"What?" Bodhi and Jasmine both asked.

I walked over to them with my notepad and pen. "You do realize we all said 'hey' at the same time, right?"

Bodhi's brows rose. "Did we really?"

"Yeah."

"Well, who wants to explain their 'hey' first?" he asked.

"I'll go," Jasmine and I both said.

Bodhi took a bite of his goulash, which had to be cold by then. "Bradly, you first."

"Okay, so we are doing all of this research, and I'm looking through these books at Jasmine's highlights and I feel like I'm going down a rabbit hole. It's interesting, but," I pointed at the ceiling, "isn't the man who wrote these books upstairs asleep in a chair? Stephen Woodruff? He's one of the City of Gleamers descendants, right? We need to save time, to help Sheena. Are you getting what I'm saying?" I sighed heavily. "Can't we just ask *him*?"

Bodhi and Jasmine glanced at each other. "Well," started Jasmine.

"You can and you can't," said a gruff voice from the top of the stairs. I noticed his feet and then his cane. It tapped each step, guiding him down.

Bodhi stood. "Mr. Woodruff? What do you mean by that?"

Mr. Woodruff sat in my seat at the pub table. "You may ask me whatever you like, but that doesn't mean I have the answer."

"But you wrote these books..." I said.

His brows rose, and the right side of his mouth curved down. Though I expected some great epiphany, he only used one finger to flip over a page of the book I jotted the highlighted notes from. Finally, he spoke. "Though I have left clues about the history of the gleamers and what is to come, I don't understand it all myself. I am certain there is a reason for that."

"But you understand what you wrote," said Jasmine from the sofa. "They are your words."

"Yes, but it is not for everyone to know or understand, and I can't break that rule."

"That's because it was for Sheena, right?" I asked as I neared him.

"I thought so, but now I realize it was only partially for her. There is something else at work here." He frowned. "Another mystery."

We waited for him to say more, but he stared ahead.

I looked away from him, my eyes landing on a passage of his book. I read aloud: "You drew out the good and allowed the wild beasts to multiply amongst those who were left."

The words made Mr. Woodruff snap out of his thoughts. "That's a twist on a verse in the book of Deuteronomy."

"What does it mean?"

"Who highlighted it?" he asked.

Jasmine raised her hand and walked over.

"Why did you highlight this?"

"Because I think I know what it means."

"Explain," he simply replied.

Jasmine pulled away a strand of hair that had found its way to her mouth. "Someone, or the Murk, drew out the good people. I think they killed them, but that part is missing. But it would make the next part make sense in regards to the Murk."

"Go on," said Mr. Woodruff.

"The people who were left would be bad or evil. They would become the wild beasts who then multiplied—a whole city or village full of them—making the Murk stronger."

I understood, also. "Instead of a City of Gleamers, there would be a city of darkness," I added.

Mr. Woodruff nodded, fixed his gaze at Jasmine, and crossed his arms. "Who would do such a thing?"

"The Murk works through people, right?" she asked.

"Yes, I know," said Mr. Woodruff.

Bodhi looked over the sofa, "Marcus."

Mr. Woodruff's eyes widened. "Son, how do you know that name?"

"Research. The name keeps coming up." He turned to me and Jasmine. "That was my 'hey' from a few minutes ago."

Mr. Woodruff shook his head and almost looked proud as he stood. "You don't need me."

"We do." I quickly read the next highlighted sentence before he could go back upstairs. "The deep trembled."

Mr. Woodruff nodded.

Tell us, I screamed inside. "Mr. Woodruff, we are running out of time. What can we do? Why isn't heaven, angels, God—why aren't we receiving any divine help when we are the good guys? Why isn't He helping us?"

"His footprints are unseen," Mr. Woodruff said as he walked away.

What? I followed him.

Mr. Woodruff turned to me as if he had heard my inner thoughts. "Dear girl, you see no panic in me, or any of the City of Gleamers. Has his steadfast love forever ceased?"

I don't know? Has it? I shrugged.

"There must be atonement." Mr. Woodruff looked up, his eyes narrowed as if he was listening for something.

"How?" I asked.

Suddenly, the whole house shook. I held onto Mr. Woodruff as we stumbled toward the stairs. He righted himself and, with a hurried limp, went to the basement window. We followed him and looked up, trying to see around Mr. Meyer's SUV tires. The ground shook again, and I lurched, grabbing onto Jasmine's arm for support.

A bright light illuminated everything outside the window. We shielded our eyes. "What's going on? What is that?" I asked.

We looked up at the ceiling, hearing a commotion above us and numerous footsteps running to one area.

Mr. Woodruff took off up the stairs as if he barely needed his cane. We followed closely behind him and found Nana and a few parents gathered at the kitchen window. Some of the others went to peer out from the family room and hallway windows.

"What's happening?" asked Jasmine.

"Here, look outside," said Ma, motioning her over and not appearing the slightest bit frightened. Bodhi and Jasmine hurried to her.

"What did you mean by atonement?" I whispered to Mr. Woodruff.

"Sacrifice."

"Hasn't Sheena already done that?"

"The one who the Murk uses," Mr. Woodruff said gravely. "He has the power to eradicate the Murk and restore balance to the world. But it comes at a great cost."

"What cost?" I demanded.

He stared at me.

"Oh... His life."

The ground shook again, and my heart pounded in my chest as I looked out the window at the men who surrounded the house. "It's not an earthquake, is it? Who are they?"

CHAPTER 26
LOGAN

We all waited to hear the bits of the puzzle we were missing about the Murk. Phoenix took a deep breath and looked around at all of us. "I don't have all the answers, but I remember glimpses of a wicked, shadowy figure who had a special connection to the Murk... He is able to control and manipulate darkness in a way that no one else can."

"What?" Cameron exclaimed.

"Now there's someone else in the mix?" asked Parker.

"I can't believe we had it all wrong." Just like most of everything we had learned thus far. There was more going on with the Murk than we knew and that had us out there running blind, making bad decisions.

It didn't take long for me to figure it out. Maybe that was the purpose of Aunt Aria's gleam. If Drake wasn't the Murk's greatest avatar, I knew exactly who it was.

"It's Marcus," I said.

Phoenix's eyes widened.

"He embodied the Murk, centuries ago, and I don't know how he's still alive. Marcus is the name he uses now."

Quincy nodded. "I've heard the name also."

"Have you seen him?" asked Phoenix.

I shook my head, not knowing how to explain Aunt Aria's gleam or if they should know about her gift at all.

The group fell into a heavy silence as they processed the information. Drake was our focus this entire time, when there was someone else. How could we have known?

"But how do we even begin to find someone like that?" Theodore asked. He sat, as if feeling the weight of the task ahead of us.

"Text Bodhi. Tell him whatever you know. His name has to come up somewhere. We have a plan. Now we need to implement it. We are almost out of time," said Corey.

"It's still the same day," said Parker.

"I don't care!" Corey said and slammed his fist against the wall. "Maybe you'll move faster if you do things as if we will run out of time in the next two hours."

I nodded. It was time to take control of the situation.

"Don't you think you need to put some clothes on?" Chana asked Phoenix. "You're coming with us."

"Oh, I guess so."

We waited.

"Are you all going to stand there watching me?"

Chana and Quincy covered their eyes. Quincy peaked through her fingers. Theodore turned her by the shoulders so that she faced the wall.

Phoenix grabbed a sweatshirt from a drawer. "You could at least step into the hall."

"Do what you have to do," said Cameron, "because we are not letting you out of our sight."

CHAPTER 27

BRADLY

Shrieks came from a few of the parents, watching the unmoving men. They were wearing long black coats and faced away from the house, strategically spaced equal distances apart. Collectively, they clasped the hand of the man to the right, briefly, and then released it.

Sheena's father was at the kitchen window. Somehow, I felt safer knowing he was there, witnessing this right along with us.

"Who are these guys?" asked Teila. "Whoa, did anyone see that?"

"See what?" several of the parents asked.

I saw it. A spark emitted from their hands when they touched. "I don't know who they are, but they are not alone. There is someone else out there. Down the street. It's kind of hard to see him. He keeps blending in with the houses. Do you see him?" He appeared as a shadow, though it was a cloudy day, so there was no light path coming from behind him for his body to obstruct in order to form a shadow (I actually paid attention to that science lesson in grade school).

Teila looked over my shoulder. "I don't see him. How do you know it's a him?"

"I don't know, but he's not moving, just watching—evaluating."

"I bet he sent them to surround us."

Although their backs were to us, I could see a slight profile of a couple of the men who formed an arc toward the front of the house. "Their faces are glowing."

"Mmm hmm..." said Mr. Woodruff, as if he already knew. He gave Sheena's dad a knowing look, and he nodded.

"You wanted help," said Mr. Woodruff as he lifted a hand toward the window. "There you go."

"That's help?" I stuttered. "Like-like-like angels?"

Mr. Woodruff glanced at me.

I guess that's a yes. "But why are they out there? And why now? Because of whoever that is down the street, skulking around the houses?" I stepped backward, away from the window, and into Teila. "Is something bad about to happen?"

Every person in the room turned, eyes darting between me and Mr. Woodruff. They wanted the answer to that question as badly as I did. In the midst of the silence, the answer came to me. What would an evil person want here with a house full of gleamers? *To steal, kill, and destroy* was my first thought. *But the way he's sneaking around, no, he's not here to confront us. That means he wants to steal, no, to take back what belongs to him.* "The Twins. Is he trying to get to them?"

Mr. Meyer shot off before we could blink and up the stairs so fast I didn't think his feet met the floor. Teila and I hurried after him.

Once we got to the room, we found Mr. Meyer just inside the door. His cell phone buzzed, but he ignored it.

The twins were sitting at the end of Sheena's grandmother's bed, looking like they had been to a spa. They wore Mrs. Meyer's robes and had towels wrapped around their heads. Their faces had color and were clearer. Despite the fading scars, I could see their beauty. If they were healthier, they could have been models.

They murmured in conversation with Seren and Ariel. Teila and I entered the room and moved all the way to the wall near the window, leaving room in front of the dresser to the left of them and the doorway across from them.

I peered down out of the window at the section of lawn between the houses. The men were still out there, surrounding us. "Can you repeat what you just whispered?" I asked the girls.

Together, as if they were one person, they turned to me. "We didn't understand," said one of them. I think she was Tiffany. "We chose a dark road, believing it would get us what we wanted. We liked it at first."

Suddenly, the whites of her eyes flashed to red and she stiffened. *Did anybody see that? Her whole countenance changed.*

She stood, and her sister stood with her. Their backs were to the door. "You know how it feels." She spoke directly to me. "You used to be one of us."

"I was never like you."

"It gave you what you wanted."

"You mean when the Murk thought all I wanted was some stupid boyfriend, which it didn't give me anyway? But you know who did figure it out? Sheena. She saw what the Murk couldn't. So you can take your lies somewhere else. God gave me what I wanted—my mom. And she's been sober for two years. The Murk had nothing to do with that." I thought for a moment. "Did you get the selfish ambition you yearned for?"

The girls' arms dropped to their sides. I didn't know what was about to happen, but something was.

Mr. Meyer took a step forward, about to position himself between us, but Ariel put her hand up as she and Seren blocked them off.

"Girl's calm down. Nothing is about to go down in this house," said Mr. Meyer.

The whites of Tiffany's, and now Alexis's, eyes turned red again.

"No!" shouted Ariel. "Fight it. Stop letting it in."

The girls lunged at Ariel and Seren as Mr. Meyer pulled at them.

I noticed movement behind them, but thought it was just someone else coming up to see what was happening. Mrs. Meyer came out of nowhere with nunchucks and hit one in the head and then the other. A quick pop, pop. She was officially my hero.

"Belinda!" exclaimed Mr. Meyer.

"Get them out of my house, Jonas, and find my child. Bring her home," she said and backed up into the hall, but still watching everything that was happening.

The twins slumped forward, holding their heads.

I raised my leg, about to kick one of them in the stomach, but Mr. Meyer stopped me. "What are you thinking? Don't do that. Tie them up."

"Why?" asked Ariel.

"Because it's trying to reinfect them. They're not strong enough to fight it off yet. For all we know, they *want* to go back. No one here is safe with them."

"You don't have to do this," said one of the twins.

"Yes, we do," Mr. Meyer sternly replied.

"Maybe we should get them out of here, like Mrs. Meyer said," said Teila.

"We might need them," said Mr. Meyer.

Seren shook her head. "They're probably just another trick of the Murk."

"Is that why the angels are here?" I asked.

"Angels where?" asked Mrs. Meyer.

I pointed at the window beside me. "They surrounded the house."

Mrs. Meyer walked over, still holding her nunchucks up. She pulled the curtain back. "I don't see anyone."

I looked outside also. There was only the snow on the side of the house, with no footprints, and the fence separating the properties. "I don't know. Everyone downstairs saw them. Maybe it was to protect us because of what the twins are capable of. Maybe we just needed to see that... Oh snap!"

"What?" asked Ariel.

"We can use them to bring the Murk back so we can get Sheena out. Maybe that's what the angels wanted us to figure out."

"Angels?" one of the girls said, looking terrified.

"Oh, you're scared now?" asked Seren. "But you're not scared of going to hell?" She leaned toward her face. "You're on the wrong team. I don't know what it's going to take for you to realize that."

CHAPTER 28

SHEENA

There was no sense of time where I was. Just an agonizing death march, each moment dragging me down deeper into this inferno. My limbs might as well have been wrapped in invisible chains. I tried to break free, but it was like wrestling with shadows—no matter how hard I fought, nothing helped.

An otherworldly game of tug-of-war took place, and I was losing big time. The only glimmer of hope was the thought that maybe, just maybe, Draven was the key to busting out of this nightmare. Somehow, together, we had to get free. At least the good part of him wanted to help me. He told me to remember what was in his journal, but it was too hard. Thinking that deeply while in excruciating pain? All I wanted to do was scream.

In my head, I played out this wild scenario of me having the ability to send out a desperate SOS of fire into the pitch-black void. A signal that screamed, "Help! Get me outta here!" Then a cavalry of angels would appear and take this thing down. But doubt crept in. If this was a boundary angels couldn't cross, as Chana said, how could they help us?

Was this the same torment the Murk used to get Draven and Phoenix to do its bidding?

I needed strength. Gritting my teeth, I summoned every ounce of willpower I had left and pushed against the invisible chains searing my skin.

As I strained, a flicker of light danced in the distance, growing brighter with each passing moment. *Is it them? Are they rescuing me?*

A surge of hope filled my heart as the light grew closer. Shadows scattered and recoiled in its presence, revealing the figure of a majestic angel. The angel's wings spread wide, radiating a golden aura that banished the surrounding darkness.

With a graceful swoop, the angel descended upon me, his face gentle and compassionate. He reached for me. His touch was cool and soothing, instantly relieving the searing pain that had consumed me for what felt like an eternity.

"Peace be still, Sheena." The angel spoke with a voice that resonated like sweet music. "You are not alone in this battle."

Tears pooled in my eyes as relief washed over me.

"Thank you." I was surprised I was even able to talk.

From the depths of my disoriented mind, I struggled to understand what was happening. Chana had always been my beacon of strength, my only hope in times of darkness, my guardian angel manifested into flesh. *Why is another angel here? Is this a vision?*

A blinding light surrounded me that I knew could only come from divine beings.

"Sheena..." As the angel spoke my name, I felt a connection I could not explain. The warmth in his voice was a comforting embrace.

"You must remain vigilant."

I mustered up the strength to ask, "Can you help me to get out of here?" My voice trembled with a mix of gratitude and fear.

Suddenly, I felt my limbs being released and breaking free. "What...what is happening?" I managed to ask, as I lifted away with him.

Our ascent seemed to take hours, but eventually, the darkness around us began to recede. We broke through the surface of it and into the light. As I looked around, I saw the remnants of a once-beautiful world.

"What you see is a result of the Murk's power."

The angel landed us gently on a hill overlooking the desolation, and I could see the pain and sadness in his eyes.

"What can I do?"

"Sheena, child of light. You hold the hope of the world. The battle is far from over. You have a long journey ahead. You hold the key in your heart. Fear not, for He is with you always. May your vision be true."

"Vision? No!" I cried. "I don't want any more visions. Either get me out of here or kill me!"

TIME REMAINING: 7 HOURS

CHAPTER 29

LOGAN

We couldn't get back to Sheena's house fast enough. None of us even slept during the ride. Suddenly, the car lost traction on a patch of black ice, careening out of control. The trees on the side of the road were a blur as the car spun, narrowly missing oncoming traffic. Drivers honked and swerved to avoid a collision. Corey frantically reached for the steering wheel, while at the same time, Theodore screamed at a pitch I wouldn't have expected from a guy.

Finally, the vehicle came to an abrupt halt facing the opposite direction. Our breaths were shaky gasps. Sweat beaded on my forehead as I frantically looked out of the windows, praying that we hadn't caused a pile-up behind us. The scent of Nana's air freshener, hanging from the rearview mirror, mingled with the faint aroma of burning rubber.

"Before anyone asks," said Theodore. "That wasn't the Murk. That was a sign that we need to stop speeding before someone gets hurt."

"Yo, are you good?" asked Corey.

"Yeah, I'll slow down." The last thing I wanted to do was wreck Nana's car.

Then came the texts from those following us.

Cameron: *Yo, what the heck!*

Justin: *Are y'all okay up there?*

I handed my phone to Corey. "Handle that, please."

We arrived at Sheena's and parked in Dingy's driveway. Not that anyone said I could. There was just nowhere else close by. As soon as I shut off the engine, Corey, Phoenix, Theodore, and I ran across the lawn and around the fence. The others followed, coming from different directions.

From the outside, the house looked peaceful. There was no sign of danger or that a dark force lurked nearby to destroy everyone inside of it.

I hurried and unlocked the side door of the Meyer's home.

Corey and I charged in, followed by Theodore, Cameron, Phoenix, and Justin. We hopped over the three stairs that led to the main floor and split up. Some of the team went down the hall to the living room, calling out to their parents. While others ran to the family room. I ran upstairs calling Uncle Jonas, and found the twins' hands tied with duct tape. An additional strip covered their mouths. A handkerchief was tied across their eyes, and headphones were over their ears.

"What happened here? What are they listening to?"

"Music that calms beasts," said Bradly. "Gospel." She and Seren sat in front of them as though they were keeping guard.

"Is there a reason they're in my room?"

She shrugged. "It was empty."

"Where is Ariel?"

Seren pointed down the hall.

Chana led the way down to Nana's room. "We've got Phoenix," she told Mr. Meyer, as we entered. He was watching Nana put anointing oil on the bedpost, dresser, windows, and door frames.

"Good. I'll be right down."

"Why is she oiling up the room?" asked Chana.

"Because of the evil that tried to manifest in here." Ariel sat in a chair, writing on a notepad. She didn't acknowledge me, nor did she need to. I was just happy to see she was okay.

"Ariel, uh, did you get to take a nap?" I asked.

She glanced up, looking weary, but determined. "Not yet," she replied and went back to writing.

"What is she working on?" I whispered to Uncle Jonas.

He shrugged. "I don't know. We will find out soon enough. "Ma Val, that's enough," he said, taking the small brown vial from her and handing it back to me without even looking.

I took it and found the cap on the dresser, twisted it on and placed the oil in my pocket.

"I'm sure your bedroom is the holiest in the house," he told her. "Where is Corey?"

"Downstairs," I replied and followed him up the hall. Chana stayed with Ariel. I stopped at Sheena's room. The door was open slightly. I almost expected her to be there, blurting out something and ending it in, "Co-bro."

I pushed the door open, seeing Aunt Belinda sitting on Sheena's bed with her eyes closed.

"Come in, Logan."

"I didn't think you saw me."

She patted the bed beside her, and I sat. Someone had cleaned the hurricane of a mess we had made of the room while searching for clues.

I studied Aunt Belinda. It was hard for everyone, but I knew that Sheena being taken was especially hard for her mother. "Can I ask you something?"

She opened her eyes. "Go ahead."

"Did what you and Uncle Jonas were going through have to do with any of this? I mean with your marriage—the arguing and stuff."

She nodded.

"Did Sheena know?"

"All that Sheena knew was that we were having problems. But, yes, it was because of my husband telling me he would no longer be Sheena's protector. I believed it was in his hands and that he could change that. I didn't want my daughter out there fighting for people with no one fighting for her. Does that make sense?"

"But we were."

"I know, but having a protector gleamer in her father gave me comfort."

I nodded in understanding.

"The problem was, he wouldn't tell her. If she didn't know, she could get into all sorts of trouble, thinking he would be there for her. Each day, I worried she'd attempt something crazy, like charging through fire, or jumping off a building to save someone, and he wouldn't appear to save her."

"I get it."

We were silent briefly, glancing around the room, focusing on nothing in particular. "I feel like I've known Sheena her whole life. She definitely would have done something crazy."

Aunt Belinda nodded and smoothed a wrinkle out of Sheena's blanket. "How are things going with Ariel?"

My eyes widened. "You know about that?"

"It's been pretty obvious."

"I'm really embarrassed right now."

"Don't be."

"I guess it's okay. It's a first for both of us. I don't know. It's not something I can think about right now—with everything going on."

She nodded. "Be delicate with her. Treat her as precious china. Love is a powerful emotion. You could probably start a battery with it," she replied with a chuckle.

"Yeah, that's funny." It really made no sense to me. But why were the hairs on my arms standing on end?

"My turn. May I ask *you* something?"

"Go ahead," I replied, just as Aunt Belinda had.

"What did Aria show you?"

"How do you know she showed me something?"

"Because I'm a mother, and I notice everything. Very little gets by me."

"I believe that." I didn't know what to say or how to say it. So instead of telling Aunt Belinda the entire story—we didn't have that kind of time anyway—I told her about the markings at the archaeological site.

"Two people, identical, but one larger than the other?" she asked.

"Yes."

"Interesting," was all she replied.

"Yo," said Corey, sticking his head into the room.

"We're ready. Everything is set."

Aunt Belinda stood. "What's set?"

"We have a plan to get Sheena back," I said, as I headed for the door.

In the hall, Nana stood against the wall. She had listened to the whole conversation.

At that moment, Ariel came running out of Nana's bedroom. "We've got it all wrong. Seren!" she called.

CHAPTER 30
LOGAN

Ariel held her phone up, and we crowded into the hall, watching. A bubbly girl with blonde hair and pink hair accessories grinned back at us. "Hey, guys! It's Marle here and I've got something exciting to share with you. Today I'm going to show you how to—"

Phoenix came up the stairs with Cameron and squeezed in beside me. "What's she got?" Then he looked at the screen. "Ariel, how do you know her?"

Ariel stopped the video. "I don't."

Phoenix's hand covered his mouth. "It's her..."

"Who is she?" I asked.

"She's one of them," said Phoenix. "She was at the camp too."

"What camp? What's going on here?" asked Aunt Belinda.

Uncle Jonas opened my bedroom door. "Get the twins to the basement. We can all watch it on the smart tv down there."

Chana and Quincy removed the duct tape from the twins, and Corey led them down the stairs. We surrounded them closely, as if they were going to make a break for it as soon as they sensed a gap of space.

When we got down to the basement, everyone found a place to sit, or stand, where they had a clear view of the television.

Ariel used the remote to find the YouTube app and typed in the video she was looking for. "Jasmine sent this to me. Actually, she might explain this better. Jasmine, do you want to—"

"No, go ahead," Jasmine replied.

"At first, I didn't think any of this concerned us. I thought it was just an influencer video like Bradly might make, but..."

Bradly pursed her lips. "Don't connect my name with this."

"You know what I mean. Just watch," Ariel replied and pressed play on the video.

Two minutes in, she stopped the video, and it froze on the girl's hand holding up a phone. The camera had zoomed in and we could clearly see what was on her phone screen.

A hush fell over the group as we exchanged concerned glances.

"Who the heck made the Murk an app?" asked Parker.

"These kids. That's what I'm trying to tell you," said Ariel. Everyone's attention was fully focused on her.

"It's worse than we thought," I said.

"Much worse," said Seren.

Ariel set the remote on the coffee table. "You still don't understand."

"Then tell us," said Quincy.

"Okay... Answer this question: what do kids want?"

Several of the Knights threw out answers: "To be understood?"

"To have friends?"

"A car?"

Justin knocked Parker on the side of his shoulder. "Can you be serious for a second?"

Ariel shook her head. "To stop the pain. I'm talking about the kids the Murk seeks. It is not about power for most," she said, looking over at the twins. "The world is full of wounded kids trying to heal and make it through each day. The Murk doesn't want that. It strengthens itself from our pain. That's why it hates gleamers; namely Sheena. We give hope."

"I'm still not—"

"Shh... Let her talk," I told Quincy.

"It has found a way to link their pain to make it stronger."

"So you're saying..."

"Yes, it wanted Sheena, but that was only part of its plan."

"What do you mean?"

"I get it," said Bodhi. "All of this has a purpose. This fight we've had with it, has been a-a distraction...to keep us busy—from the bigger picture."

Ariel nodded. "Exactly. The Murk is after something more than just one gleamer. Yes, it wants to destroy both Sheena and us, because we've created a problem for it." Ariel placed a hand behind her back and with the other, acted out holding a sword by its hilt and dueling in the air. "While it's fighting us on this end," she wiggled the fingers of the hand behind her back, "we are blind to what's happening on the other side. It's been working out a whole other plan. It's trying to harness the pain of all these kids and create a whole bigger problem," she explained.

Cameron's eyebrows furrowed. "But how does this involve the app?"

"The app is how it is getting to these kids," replied Ariel. "It's like a portal for the Murk to enter their lives and manipulate their pain."

"It's a virtual reality game," Phoenix replied, his eyes focused on the screen. "But it's not just any game." A flicker of recognition crossed his face. His eyes widened, and he turned to me with a sense of urgency. I was sure he was suddenly remembering something.

"The app...it was created by a company called ICOUPTech. They're known for their cutting-edge technology and immersive simulations."

"Wait," said Quincy. "ICOUPTech? That's the same company responsible for those controversial experiments a few years back, right?"

Phoenix nodded solemnly. "Yes, they were conducting experiments using virtual reality as a means of therapy for trauma victims. But rumors started swirling that they were pushing the boundaries too far, delving into dangerous territory."

I mulled over their words. "So this is actually the Murk's company?"

"The Murk controls whoever owns it."

"The things we uncover when we start searching," Stephen Woodruff sang to himself, as though he didn't have a care in the world.

"Okay," said Corey. "This is a lot to take in. What you're saying is the Murk is using technology as a weapon, harnessing the emotions of these unsuspecting kids to kill their hope and feed its own power."

"But why do they stay in that place? That place of pain and despair?" asked Parker. "I mean, we all experience pain sometimes, but staying there is the problem."

Cameron shook his head. "Dude, Romans 6:16. 'You become the slave of whatever you choose to obey. Choose evil, you become the slave of evil. Choose good' —you get the point."

"Stop being so deep," said Theodore. "You get what Parker is trying to say."

I faced Parker. "You're right. A bit of pain and despair isn't necessarily wicked. It's what they can evolve into if left unchecked that's the problem.

"Okay, that's all well and good, but how do we shut it down?" asked Phoenix.

"That's what we need to figure out," said Seren. "But first, we need to get Sheena back."

"You have to think like a person trying to hide something," said Jasmine as if she were thinking aloud. "I would use virtual private networks to mask my IP data."

"She's right. Wait, I've got it... A virus," said Bodhi. "Malware. How many kids are thinking about anti-virus software, especially on their phones?"

"So we get them to download the malware, thinking it's something else, right?" asked Jasmine.

"Bodhi nodded."

"You can do that?" I asked.

"Umm... I know things. I'll leave it at that."

As the group continued to discuss our next steps—how quickly this could be done, how many kids would download it, and taking turns resting, a loud crash suddenly echoed from outside the house. Corey was the first to the window. "I can't see anything from down here," he muttered, peering out.

Pushing past him, I dashed upstairs, and some of the others followed. By the time we reached the kitchen, several of the parents were already looking outside.

"What's going on?" I asked, as I joined them.

We looked over the fence. Dingy's back door was wide open and all the windows of the house were blown out.

"Marcus," said Mr. Woodruff.

"I think we can handle whoever this Marcus person is," said Parker. "We have a house stuffed with Gleamers. Twenty or so."

"That's not enough."

CHAPTER 31

LOGAN

"Everyone stay here. I'm going over there. Lock the door behind me and don't unlock it unless you're certain it's me," said Uncle Jonas.

"Don't you have to stay with Dingy?" asked Chana.

"I'll go," I told them.

"Me too," said Theodore.

"You stay here. No offense, Theodore, I need gleamers," said Uncle Jonas.

"But we're the Knights of the Gleam."

"Yes, and that means we can't all go over there and leave everyone else here without help," I told him.

Theodore nodded in understanding.

"I'll go," said Phoenix.

"But you could—"

"I'll take that chance."

Stephen Woodruff stepped forward with his cane. "I'm in."

I didn't know what his gleam was, or how he thought he could help, but I wasn't about to argue with him.

Then Corey stepped forward.

"Uh-uh…Corey, what are you doing?" asked Cameron. "He said gleamers, not Knights of the Gleam."

Corey zipped his coat. "We are all walking around like we have forever to save Sheena. For the hundredth time, we are running out of time. If we are going to do this. We have to do this now."

Cameron grabbed his arm. "Wait. I know you. What's going on? Why won't you look me in the eye? What are you not telling me?"

Corey's eyes bore into the floor, avoiding Cameron. He still couldn't find the words to tell his cousin his secret. He glanced at me, and in his expression I saw his desperation for assistance. So I did as any friend would. Time was ticking away, and there was no room for a lengthy conversation. "Corey is a gleamer. He found out recently. Let's go."

Corey's head snapped at me. "Yo, did I ask you to say that?"

Cameron's eyes were wide, but his voice stayed calm. "Who else knows?"

Corey turned to the door. "Can we talk about this later?"

Cameron's voice rose. "No. Who else knows?"

"Just Logan and Theodore until now—thanks for that, Logan."

"We just found out today when he saved us," said Theodore.

"From what? What did you do?"

"Was I there?" asked Justin.

"'Ephesians 4:25, 'So stop telling lies. Let us tell our neighbors the truth, for we are all parts of the same body.'"

"Here he goes with the scriptures."

"All you had to do was tell me the truth. I mean, we're always together."

"Well, how about this scripture: John 8:32, 'And you will know the truth, and the truth will set you free.'"

"Oh, so you're mocking me now."

"Let's go," said Mr. Woodruff, pushing past us. Uncle Jonas was already outside.

"I wasn't mocking you. I was giving you back what you were giving me."

"Hey, I can't help that I'm a pastor's kid. I didn't choose this life. This life chose me."

"Just like being a gleamer," said Corey. "I didn't choose it. Neither did Sheena."

They were silent for a moment. Corey's words seemed to make Cameron think.

"I'm sorry," said Corey.

"I'm pretty sure you're not sorry. Go," he said and pressed through the group to get away from the door.

"Seren, you too. Let's go," I told her.

"I'm in. I've got you. Whatever you need," she replied as she grabbed her coat. "I'll be right back, Ariel."

"Remember," said Stephen Woodruff. "Your fear strengthens it. If you are afraid, you're safer here." He was looking directly at Phoenix when he said it.

I spoke up for him. "He's good. You're good, right?"

Phoenix nodded and walked outside.

The six of us left the house like hobbits on a journey to Mount Doom. The air was dry and cold, but none of us pulled on our hoods or tightened our coats around us. I realized that most of us were protector gleamers, which was fitting. Our combined strengths might save us from whatever we were about to face. We walked along the fence to the other side and crossed the snow covered driveway where I had parked Nana's car.

The storm door slammed against the house and remained open. We stopped there, on the back steps. Uncle Jonas looked inside the door and motioned for us to follow him. Stephen Woodruff used his cane and hopped up each step.

"Wait, Mr. Woodruff. I think you should stay here."

He raised a brow. "You do?"

"Things may get a little messy in there. I'll call you in when it's safe."

He shrugged and leaned against the house. "Okay."

The entrance opened to a great room. Stairs wrapped around to a loft area above us.

"You see that?" whispered Phoenix.

"Yeah, I do," I replied. A figure stood in the shadows at the top of the stairs.

Suddenly, the door slammed shut behind us and the scattered shards of the broken windows seamlessly pieced themselves back together, sealing us inside.

I tried the door. "We're locked in."

CHAPTER 32

SHEENA

In the pitch-black realm of the Murk, where every sound echoed with a haunting resonance and every breath tasted of ash, I trembled. I couldn't believe what I was hearing. A vision. I knew it; I'd been through it before, the harrowing plunge into the unknown, where reality and dreams blurred at their edges. But this time was different. I wanted it to be real so badly—to finally be free of the Murk and the torment.

"Sheena, listen closely, but don't wake up. Not yet."

"Chana?"

"The Knights of the Gleam are about to encounter something they are not ready for."

"Send their guardians."

"You know I have no control over what their guardians do."

"Who is it?"

"Corey, Logan, Phoenix, Seren, and Stephen Woodruff."

"Stephen Woodruff?" I repeated in shock.

"Yes, many gleamers have come together to figure out a way to bring you back."

"No one can save me," I said sadly. My fate seemed sealed, and there was no hope for me now.

"Have you forgotten all you were just told by the archangel? Sheena, snap out of it." Her voice was stern and commanding.

I felt a sting across my face. "Did you just slap me?"

"We only have seconds left. The Knights are not strong enough for this."

"What can I do? I'm so weak."

"Where you are weak, He is strong. Look inside yourself."

"I can't."

"Sheena, your father is with them."

"What?"

Immediately, screaming filled my ears. It came from all around me. My eyes shot open. The burning was intense, but I honed in on the voices. It was my friends. I listened, trying to figure out what was happening. How could I hear them? Were they close...close enough to touch? Was this another trick? It couldn't be. Chana had just warned me they needed my help. I groaned inside, feeling more of my life zapping away. What could I possibly do? I listened and prayed. *I have to save them somehow or at least give them enough time to get away.*

Immediately, somewhere deep inside, I felt stronger. Something pressed against my back and pushed me forward. "What is that?"

"Not what, but who..."

"Draven? Are you there?"

"Grab hold," was all he replied.

CHAPTER 33
LOGAN

The figure emerged from the shadows—the embodied manifestation of the Murk. His eyes glinted as he studied us with cool detachment.

"Why is it over here?" asked Corey.

"Because it couldn't get past the angels next door," said Uncle Jonas.

"I see you all have come to play," he said with a mocking smirk. "But I am only here for the child."

"What child? There are no children here," said Uncle Jonas.

"Hmm...If that's how you want to play it. Let the games begin."

"Where is Sheena?" demanded Seren, her fists clenched at her sides. Uncle Jonas pushed her behind him.

"Ah, so impatient," replied the man. "The accent...Scottish. I remember you. You'll have to do better than that if you want to save her." He glanced at his fingernails as if he were examining their shine. "There's no easy way to tell you this." He sighed and then dropped his hand. "Sheena Meyer is mine."

"You can't have her," said Corey, stepping forward.

The man chuckled. "Oh, I'm afraid I already do, boy, as well as others. And soon, she'll be one of us."

"Not if we stop you," I said, feeling a surge of energy run through my veins.

The man's smile faded, and his eyes narrowed. "You underestimate me, Logan Tobias," he said as he stepped closer to the banister of the loft. "But I like your spirit. It will make it all the more satisfying when I destroy it."

I don't like it using my name. I had never heard the Murk say any name but Sheena's. What was worse, he said it as if he knew me.

His facial features changed before my eyes and I recognized him—the man from the archeological site. The same snarl, the same sinister satisfaction in his eyes, reveling in the act of something evil.

As if on cue, a deafening roar echoed through the house. The back door burst open, tearing off its hinges with a force that made me stagger.

Before any of us could react, with the flick of his wrist, he summoned lava-like tendrils that wrapped around us, lifting us off our feet and suspending us in the air. "Now, let's have some fun," he said, as he toyed with us, the tendrils winding tighter and tighter, burning, and sending jolts of electricity through us.

I struggled against them, but it was no use. They were too strong, and I could feel my energy draining with each passing moment. The man smirked at me, enjoying my helplessness. Then I noticed, though it attacked us all, I was the one it pulled toward him.

"Let him go!" yelled Seren, her hands glowing with white light.

The man only laughed. "I don't think so, my dear. We'll have plenty of time to play with him once we take care of the rest of you. Or... You can just bring me the child."

"That's not going to happen," said Uncle Jonas. His hands began to glow and a bright blue force shot out towards the man.

The Murk growled and released us. It turned its attention towards Uncle Jonas. Corey took the opportunity to run and topple me over, out of the way of another tendril.

"Are you all right?" he asked.

"Yeah, I'm good," I said, as we stood watching Uncle Jonas slice through another tendril with his sword of energy, freeing Seren. She promptly placed a protective field around him while he freed Phoenix.

Another tendril came at us and we dove to the side. I rolled over and scrambled to my feet, determined to demonstrate the might of my gleam. Yet, before I could unleash it, another tendril snaked around me and trapped my arms to my sides, coiling tighter than the first.

Suddenly, a voice yelled out from behind us: "Gleamers, defy this evil!"

The man scoffed. "Well, if it isn't Stephen Woodruff, come to save the day."

Mr. Woodruff stepped forward, his eyes glowing. "Release them. Now."

He laughed. "You'll have to do better than that, Stephen. You are no match for me."

"I may not be, but the gleam is, Marcus."

It seemed startled to hear that name.

"It is more powerful than you will ever be." Mr. Woodruff spread his arms wide and focused his gaze. Instantly, a bright light filled the room, forcing Marcus to shield his eyes.

And then, from the corner of my eye, I saw movement that wasn't him. A glimpse of purple hair. I couldn't believe my eyes. It was Sheena.

She slowly crept in through the wall, like she was coming from another dimension. Smaller versions of those giant tendrils attached to her. With one quick move, she stepped forward and grabbed Marcus from behind, struggling to keep him in her grasp.

"Sheena!" Uncle Jonas screamed.

"Get out of here!" She shouted.

We used the distraction to break free from the grip of those tendrils, and with a collective shout, we charged forward.

The light of our gleams burned brightly. We were doing it—about to recover Sheena. Fueled by the adrenaline surging within me at the prospect of saving her, I felt invincible.

But as we were about to make out next move, Phoenix abruptly ran up, cutting us off. He raised his hands forward and shot a force toward Sheena.

My thoughts of triumph came to a screeching halt. A scream escaped me as she vanished before my eyes.

"What did you do?" yelled Seren.

Uncle Jonas's mouth was open in shock and his face contorted with a mixture of rage and grief. He let out a deep, heart-wrenching cry and raised his sword of energy, ready to strike down the boy responsible for letting the Murk snatch Sheena out of our grasp.

In one swift motion, Uncle Jonas swung, the force of his blow strong enough to shatter bones. But instead of slicing through Phoenix, the energy seized the wall, creating an opening clear through to the other side. He fell to his knees and released another cry that echoed through every corner of the house. A sound that mirrored all the pain and anguish I had held inside since losing Sheena to the Murk. And in that moment, it felt like the very foundation of our world was crumbling beneath us.

If I didn't know better, I'd swear time just hit pause. I was afraid to speak and afraid not to. If Uncle Jonas didn't attack Phoenix, Corey might. He took a step toward him.

I jumped in front of him. "Wait, wait!"

"Corey... Uncle Jonas, it wasn't on purpose. He missed. Right Phoenix? You were aiming for Marcus and missed? Is that what happened?" I asked, trying to make myself believe it as much as them. "You were afraid of that-that monster?"

Phoenix stared at me. His expression was like ice, distant and detached. "How can I be afraid of the monster when I am the monster?" he said and backed away, the whites of his eyes flashing red.

"Why are you acting like Drake?" asked Corey.

"I'm not acting like Drake. I *am* Drake." He turned and went up to exactly where Marcus had stood on the loft and walked right into the Murk and disappeared.

Corey's hands flew to his head. "Yo, this is the guy you trusted. Are you kidding me?"

"But he-he's a Knight...I-I don't know what's happening right now." A rush of heat surged from my collar, setting my ears ablaze.

Corey shook me. "Snap out of it. No fear, remember?"

"We made a terrible mistake," I replied.

Seren pointed accusingly at me. "You! You made a mistake."

Corey helped Stephen Woodruff up from the floor, where he had collapsed from expending so much energy. Seren handed him his cane.

The house now felt like just a house, rather than a portal to a place unimaginable. And it left me feeling like I had just awakened from a horrible dream.

"Sheena?" Uncle Jonas whispered, his voice barely audible, as if he tried one last time, she would reappear. He looked up along the walls of the loft. She didn't.

Corey went to Uncle Jonas. "We saw her," he said. "And she helped us. She's still Sheena. We can get to her in time. I know we can. We *will* get her home."

"All right," Uncle Jonas finally replied, his voice steady. "Let's do just that."

CHAPTER 34

SHEENA

An ear-splitting roar encircled me, causing my bones to vibrate. The Murk was enraged and made sure I felt its intensity. Daggers pierced my skin. At least that's what they felt like. The pain would only cause me to want to "give up the ghost," as I heard one of Nana's church friends say once. What would it benefit from killing me?

I didn't know how he did it, but Draven pushed me through, and though I couldn't free myself, I got a glimpse of my father and friends and was able to help them. I did just as Draven said, and grabbed hold, not knowing I would end up pulling Marcus away from them. The strength that filled me as I fought for them still lingered.

"Sheena..." Amid my internal screams was a voice. Trying to find me. Not yelling, but searching.

I focused all my energy on that voice, trying to respond but unable to form any words. Suddenly, everything went black.

When I awoke, the Murk was no longer writhing around me. I was in a dark room with no windows or doors. A single light swung back and forth over my chair.

I wasn't fooled. This was just an illusion, like the others.

My hands were tied behind my back, and my legs were bound with thick ropes. My head throbbed and my body ached. But despite all that, I was relieved to be away from the Murk's grasp if only for a moment before whatever was going to happen next.

A figure appeared in front of me.

"Who are you?" I asked, struggling against my restraints.

The figure moved closer and lowered his hood. I recognized his jet black hair and piercing eyes.

"Marcus," I said.

"It was foolish of you to interfere. Where did it get you?"

"Why have you brought me here? You didn't need an illusion to tell me that."

"No, but I wanted your full attention. You have been chosen," Marcus replied cryptically. "Chosen by the Murk to be its vessel."

"Why? Is it not happy with you?"

He ignored my words. "You'll be one of many. A holder—a guardian of its qualities. That's the role of a vessel. Simple."

A chill ran down my spine. Then I giggled and my giggle turned to spiteful laughter.

Marcus watched me amusingly. "Why do you laugh?"

"Light and darkness cannot exist in the same place."

"Yet here we are."

"Good and evil cannot join together."

"But it will."

"No, it won't. In case you didn't know, it's already written. We win."

He tapped my forehead and in an instant, I was back in the desert as Phillip, staring into a man's eyes. This same man's eyes. His hands choked my neck as Professor Pembly pulled at his arms.

I grabbed at his wrists, trying to pull them away as I gasped for air. "I see you," he said.

Immediately, I was back in the dark room.

"You were there, weren't you? How did you get there? Is there a traveler among you?"

If he didn't know about Aunt Aria's gleamer gift, he sure wasn't going to find out from me. I looked him in the eyes, but I didn't respond.

"Not to worry. We will break you and you will tell all you know. But for now, how did you do that?"

"Do what?"

"How did you break free and come after me?"

The room filled with the scent of burning embers. "How are you still alive after so many years?" I asked.

"Do not test me, girl!" Marcus growled. "You don't know my power."

He came closer and I could feel the heat of his anger radiating off him. But I also noticed something else. Fear.

"You're afraid of the future," I said, looking directly into his eyes. "The gleam knows what's coming and that scares you."

"The gleam knows nothing," a voice behind me snapped.

He slowly walked around me into view and stooped to my eye level.

"Phoenix? No... How?"

Drake appeared next and the three of them stood side by side before me, like an unholy trinity.

A sinister grin crept across Marcus's face. "These two do not need to be tied to darkness any longer," said Marcus. "But it must have you. You can release them. Give in, and it will all be over quickly."

"We tried that already. It was supposed to release him," I said looking in Drakes direction, "in exchange for me. It lied."

"Only the foolish trusts evil. What is your choice, girl?" he demanded.

I didn't know what to do and couldn't think of a way to stall.

"Sheena Meyer!"

"I'm thinking!"

"I wish we had more time, but we don't. Therefore, we will ensure that this occurs expeditiously."

The hairs on my neck stood on end as I realized what they were going to do. I had to act now, and hope my friends and family were working to get me out, like Chana said. I didn't want to endure another moment in this place. *God, please help me*, I prayed inside.

Marcus backed up, and Drake and Phoenix came closer.

"Do you remember trying to reach me?" I said, looking directly into Phoenix's eyes and then Drakes. "You both were trying to get out."

Phoenix instantly dropped his gaze. Then he and Drake chuckled. "Sentimental fool."

"'Greater is he who is within me than he that is within the world!'" I screamed, before I felt a force crashing down on me.

TIME REMAINING: 4 HOURS

CHAPTER 35

LOGAN

We trailed behind Uncle Jonas. A palpable tension hung in the air, as heavy as the snow-laden clouds above. With shoulders tense and fists clenched at his sides, he strode away from Dingy's house. I don't think he even felt the cold. Each stride labored, weighted by suppressed rage. He was a tightly wound coil, ready to snap.

I lagged back, not wanting to feel the brunt of his pain.

Stephen Woodruff held the door open for me. Everyone was already inside when I approached. "Be of good courage," he told me.

My head hung low. An inevitable reproach awaited the boy who trusted Phoenix. I could already hear the conversations starting inside. Down the hall, Uncle Jonas didn't stop walking. I don't think he even saw of heard anyone.

Phoenix's words echoed in my head. *He is Drake? Why did he say that?*

"What happened?" asked Cameron. "You're clothes are burnt."

"Phoenix is gone," said Seren in passing. "Where can I go to clean up? That thing touched me. I hope I can fit some of Sheena's clothes."

"Thing? What touched her?" asked Quincy.

Corey was still taken aback. "I'm still trying to understand. We take him with us for help, and he rejoins that thing?"

"Him who?" asked Cameron.

"Phoenix. The Murk took him," I replied. And walked away.

"What?"

"Logan, where are you going?" asked Bradly.

I stopped. "I don't care about Phoenix right now. The Murk can have him, chew him up, and spit him out. Good riddance."

"You don't mean that," said Ariel.

"Yeah, I do. Everything we do makes us lose focus on what we're supposed to be doing, which is getting Sheena back. Phoenix is just another distraction."

"Whoa, why are you turning on him?" asked Justin. "You really don't care?"

I sighed, turning away from the group and stared out the window. There were no angels out there or any sign of the Murk. Just all of our footprints in the snow. The Knights couldn't see the emotion on my face, but I hated myself for rejecting Phoenix so callously.

I walked back over to them and lowered my voice. "Can we just stick with the plan?"

Corey studied me. "You mean using that find-a-phone app to locate Sheena's phone?"

"Yeah. She has her phone. If the tracker works, we can determine where the Murk is. Sheena's mom has the app."

"Then what?" asked Parker.

"The Trojan horse."

"Yeah," said Corey, "but I'm going to need to change into one of your sweatsuits first." The Murk's force had burned clear through his pant legs, but his skin was untouched.

The Knights didn't know it, but the Trojan horse was already happening—in order to spare their lives.

CHAPTER 36
THEODORE

"They're back," Justin called. He came upstairs where I was sitting with Dingy. His towering figure cast an intimidating shadow over me, reminiscent of a grizzly bear asserting its dominance. My heart pounded in my chest as I sat up and rubbed the sleep from my eyes. When you haven't slept for twenty-four hours, sleep has a way of nearly putting you in a chokehold until you give in.

"This is no time to hurkle-durkle," Seren said from behind him and walked into the ensuite.

"What is she talking about? I don't know what that means," I groaned, looking around, disoriented.

"It's a Scottish thing," said Chana, joining us. "She thinks you're being lazy."

"Wait, that was Seren? They're back?"

"That's what I just told you," said Justin. "Come on."

I hurried after him to the basement where the Knights gathered, listening to Corey's account of what occurred at Dingy's house. The shock of it all was still in his voice.

"I knew it!" I kept repeating. "I knew! I told you!"

"Theodore, stop. Relax," Chana said, reaching for me.

I pulled away. I couldn't relax and wondered why she was being so calm about what she had heard.

I should have gone with them. They actually saw Sheena, and she saved them. Chana and I exchanged glances when Corey told us that part. "You mean you didn't try to grab her or anything?"

"Did you not hear what happened to us? She was nowhere near us."

The whole ordeal confused me. It just didn't make sense. In the past few hours, off and on, I wanted to beat the crap out of both Logan and Phoenix. Even though, eventually, deep inside, I wasn't so sure Phoenix was to blame for Sheena being taken like I had originally thought. For the sake of our team, I took the understanding route. Phoenix didn't want to relive what he went through with the Murk. Got it. He was terrified to face it again. Understood. Been there. Although, Phoenix experienced that evil to a greater degree and for a longer period than I did.

Now he was back inside the Murk, proving he was exactly who I first thought he was. A snake.

"Psst, Logan..." I waved him over. He'd been moping around. I wasn't sure if it was because of Phoenix or what we were about to face. Bradly, Quincy, and I had the hardest part of the plan, but I chose not to think about it and to definitely not share it with my parents.

Logan only lifted a hand and shook his head. I guess he wasn't ready to talk.

I paced the basement floor, rounding the pool table for the second time. I couldn't shake the feeling that there was more to the story than we understood. There was something about the whole situation that didn't sit right with me. I played out Corey's narrative over and over in my head. We were missing something important.

Justin, seated in one of the folding chairs, leaned forward, elbows bent on his knees. His eyes were dark and somber. "Corey, you keep saying that you saw Sheena. But how do we know that wasn't just your imagination? The Murk—it plays tricks on your mind. It can make you see things that aren't there."

Was that what we were missing? That it wasn't really Sheena? I stopped pacing and faced the group.

Corey's eyes narrowed. "You think that was some mind trick? I saw Sheena, and she saved us. I know what I saw."

Justin sighed and shook his head. "Okay. Then it's settled. What are we going to do with the twins?"

"They're coming with us. They're the Plan B," said Corey.

TIME REMAINING: 2 HOURS

CHAPTER 37
LOGAN

I hesitated outside Sheena's parents' bedroom. The door, ajar and creaking softly, was a foreboding gateway to the inevitable confrontation ahead. Her mother's bergamot essential oils wafted out, laced with the distant aroma of bacon that someone had eaten in the bedroom—scents that had always been comforting, now serving only to heighten my anxiety. The weight of the unavoidable conversation bore down on my shoulders with an almost physical force. I needed to step inside, to face the music as they say, but each second that ticked by was a second longer that I could delay seeing their faces crumble under disappointment—disappointment in me.

Corey and Justin came out of my bedroom, following Bradly and Quincy with the twins.

"You ready?"

"Uh, yeah," I replied and pointed into Sheena's parents' bedroom.

Corey nodded, and I walked inside and cleared my throat. "We, uh, we're leaving now."

Uncle Jonas didn't even acknowledge me as he came out of the ensuite drying his hand on a towel.

Aunt Belinda stopped him. "Where are you going?"

"With them," he replied and tossed the towel into the bathroom.

"No, you're not," Dingy's mother replied, walking over from the other side of the room with her arms folded across her chest. It was the first I had heard from her other than speaking to Dingy while keeping him comfortable in the sitting area of Sheena's parents' bedroom. "If you're not here, who is going to protect my son?"

"I don't have to be here for that. You're new to this and have no idea what I'm capable of. Dingy is safe here. I have to go and bring my daughter back home. You should understand that."

"No." She pointed at me. "*They* have to get her back. That's what they are called to do. You are called to protect my son."

Aunt Belinda watched them closely while picking up the towel and setting it on the counter.

"You already disappeared with him once. Here I am at home thinking my son is safe in bed, when he's out there, nine years old, and trying to fight crime or whatever it is they do."

"Don't act like the rest of the world out there who don't know gleamers exist. You know exactly what they do," said Aunt Belinda. "You are well aware of what a gleamer is and their mandate."

"Hold on," Uncle Jonas interrupted and pointed at his chest. "Did I disappear with him, or did he disappear on his own, and then I went after him? There's a difference."

Dingy's mother shook her head as it dropped. "He's so young."

"I agree...and I promise you, if he needs me, I will be here in a split second. We're connected that way. But my daughter is out there with only hours left. I need to bring her home."

"Go," said Dingy, not looking up from the game he played on his mother's phone. "Sheena needs you right now. It's killing her."

All eyes locked on Dingy. Was he assuming that, or did he know? Being that he was the true Angelus Bellator, I had to believe he knew.

I held my hand out, and Aunt Belinda handed me her phone. We all knew the plan. I turned to leave without another word.

"Logan..." said Uncle Jonas. "I don't blame you—regarding Phoenix."

I sighed in relief, feeling a bit lighter as I walked out of the room and descended the stairs. I faltered on the bottom step as I caught sight of the City of Gleamers descendants huddled together in the living room. A few looked at me with solemn expressions, their hands tightly intertwined as if seeking comfort from one another.

As I made my way down into the foyer, they all turned their attention to me. Uncle Jonas and Aunt Belinda followed me, their footsteps loud against the sudden stillness of the house. They urged me towards Nana, who stood front and center, her arms outstretched towards me like a guiding light. I walked into her embrace, her whispered words sending shivers down my spine.

"We won't be far," she said, her voice quivering with emotion. How did they know where we would be when we didn't even know ourselves? I could only nod in silent acceptance as uncertainty washed over me.

Nana pulled back and looked into my eyes. "There are things within our knowledge that we are unable to disclose. You may question why we cannot reveal it to you, but permission is required before we can share this information. Do you understand?"

"Yes, Ma'am." I nodded, understanding that there were rules and limitations to what heaven allowed the descendants of the City of Gleamers to reveal. It was frustrating at times, not knowing everything about our situation, but I also trusted them. Specifically Nana.

Aunt Aria moved forward. "Remember, what you saw was real and true. It's important."

"I will," I replied. It was as if they were giving me instructions before sending me off on a dangerous quest, with no guarantee of return.

"May your vision be true," they all said in unison. Each gleamer placed a hand on my shoulder as if transferring their strength to me. Nana's grip tightened, and I could feel the power coursing through me from their collective gleam. Then they all spoke:

"By light we rise, by faith we thrive,
In gleaming hearts, our strength is alive.
Through shadowed paths, we boldly tread,
With God's light, our purpose spread.
In every trial, we shall stand,
Guided by the Maker's hand.
With gifts divine, our souls alight,
In God's grace, we find our might.
For in the darkness, we shall gleam,
A beacon bright, a radiant dream.
United, steadfast, we'll endure,
In God's light, forever pure."

I locked eyes with Mr. Knight and saw his hope reflected back at me, while Stephen Woodruff nodded in approval. "You are one of us, Logan. A Tobias. Descendant of Phillip Tobias, the man whose grandfather brought our ancestors together many years ago. That is who you are. You will carry on in your grandfather's stead after we are long gone."

Their hands fell away and Aunt Aria handed me Draven's worn leather journal, its pages filled with faded ink and delicate sketches. I strode through the dining room and butler's pantry and stopped. All of the parents were there in the kitchen and family room. Their eyes filled with a mixture of worry and hope.

Standing in the hall and seated at the kitchen banquette, my team waited.

"Let's go," I said. We stepped outside into the cold air. As the door closed behind us, a hush fell over the neighborhood, as if the entire city was aware of the gravity of what we were about to face. I glanced up at the starry sky, seeking solace. But tonight, even the stars seemed to hold their breath, their gentle glow reminding me of the secrets they held behind them.

"Don't worry, we're ready," said Corey. I knew he was trying to figure out where my thoughts were, because I was so quiet, but I was far from worried. I was torn between wanting to protect them, making them stay put, and wanting to lead them into battle. It's what I beat myself up for not doing with Sheena. But they didn't need a father right now, forbidding them from leaving the house. They needed a leader, someone strong enough to take charge and make tough decisions. The leader Corey effortlessly was—that I struggled to be.

I glanced at Ariel. I couldn't take seeing disappointment on her face again. I wanted her to be proud of what I was about to do. "We are the Knights of the Gleam...."

Quincy looked away.

"The rest of you are part of our team. You've helped us get this far and nothing you've done has gone unnoticed: Chana, Quincy, and Seren."

Quincy glanced at me, and I couldn't be sure, but I thought I saw a tear in her eye. Seren nodded, arm in arm with Ariel.

And Chana... She didn't have to express anything. She was an angel, after all, and in this matter, could do no more than we could do. She had told me and Ariel that angels couldn't go to that place. That left her as helpless as we all were.

"You all know what cars you are riding in. Quincy, Bradly, and Theodore, stay together." I took Aunt Belinda's phone from my pocket and got to work on finding Sheena's location. Actually, all I had to do was tap on her app. It hadn't been twenty-four hours yet, so if Sheena's phone was fully charged when she left, it might still have some juice.

A few seconds passed. The screen flickered and glowed. Suddenly, a ping indicated that the app had successfully located Sheena's phone.

Corey and I exchanged determined glances as the phone's screen zoomed in, displaying an exact location. "Let's go," said Corey.

I opened the driver's side door of Nana's car. Theodore, Quincy, and Bradly rode in the backseat. To my surprise, Ariel got into the front passenger seat, having exchanged cars with Chana. She waved at Seren and glanced over at me. I don't know why, but I needed her—to have her close—to have her support, but I didn't know how much until that moment.

We pulled away from the house and headed up Strong Avenue to Third Street. Following the map, Shoreline Drive would take us up to U.S. Route 31 and away from the city.

The road stretched out before us, illuminated only by the occasional streetlights we passed. The caravan pressed on. We were the lone cars on the road, as if the world knew what was about to happen and retreated to safety. I glanced in the rearview mirror at Theodore, Quincy, and Bradly in the back seat. They all looked straight ahead. We were a silent vessel of determination.

Our instructions were clear about the roles we would play when we arrived. I didn't know about anyone else, but I refused to believe we were coming back without Sheena. I set my resolve on saving her. I glanced at the map on the phone in my hand and pulled off the road. A hush fell over the car as if we'd been talking. Maybe it was because each of us was holding our breath, realizing what we were about to face.

"We're here," I said, showing Ariel the phone. I shut the car off as the others pulled in beside ours, on the shoulder of the road. The moon cast a soft glow upon the field in front of us, as if it knew exactly where we needed to go.

Ariel looked out of her window. "But there's nothing out here."

CHAPTER 38

LOGAN

Doors slammed shut as we got out of our cars and looked beyond the wooden rail fence at a snow covered field.

"This is it?" asked Parker, calmer and quieter than I was used to him being.

"We should get moving," said Cameron. "We only have about an hour."

"Trust me on this. We need to proceed with caution," I replied, trying to convey both confidence and concern in equal measure.

The air crackled with energy, and I hesitated for only a moment before crossing the threshold, throwing my leg over the fence. I almost thought that when I stepped onto the snow on the other side, I would materialize in another dimension.

Jasmine held up her phone. "I've got the county records."

"How does that help us?" asked Theodore.

"I thought you would want to know who this property is registered to."

"You were able to pinpoint this property?"

"It wasn't hard. The same person owns every parcel around us. There's some kind of camp here."

My eyes widened. "One of the Murk camps?"

"I don't know, but we should be prepared for that."

"Corey, are your boys coming?" asked Parker.

"No. Not that they didn't want to. They're not afraid of this stuff."

"Why not?" asked Teila.

"Where I'm from, we've seen the devil. In the drug dealers, the violence, and everything else that plagues the hood. Don't get me wrong, there are good people there too, but after what we've seen, this stuff doesn't scare us so much. We already know of the evils of the world. But whoever is running all of this, I mean controlling what we do: angels or heaven, it has allowed them to not only see, but remember everything they have helped us with. That tells us they are part of the larger scheme of things. But this—I didn't want to bring anyone into this but the Knights. Everything that happens is on us."

"Understood," Teila replied and helped move the Twins along.

"Who *does* owns the property?" asked Chana.

"Marcus. Marcus Ahmad."

"That's the guy that attacked us at Dingy's house," said Seren. "We're at the right place, all right."

At that, everyone stepped over the fence. I put my hands out in case I had to assist Ariel, but she didn't need me.

"It feels like a ghost town out here—or ghost field. Does anyone see anything?" asked Parker. "We shouldn't use flashlights. If it doesn't know we're here, we sure don't want to alert it."

"He's right," said Theodore.

Suddenly, a dog came sprinting past. Some of us jumped back.

"What was that? A wolf? A coyote?" asked Parker.

"A scout," murmured one of the twins. But I think I was the only one who paid attention.

"Calm down. It was a dog. That way," said Corey.

"Why?" I asked.

"It's running from something. Whatever that something is, is about to deal with us." Corey patted my shoulder. "Let's go."

We cautiously followed the path that the dog had taken, seeing its footprints in the snow. It was a good thing nights were brighter in the winter.

We moved silently. The air grew colder with each step we took. Unease settled in the pit of my stomach. What were we going to find when we got there? Wherever *there* was.

It was as if the entire property was holding its breath, waiting for us to stumble upon its secrets. Trees surrounded us in the distance, and the only sound that accompanied our footsteps was the wind.

Suddenly, a low growl echoed around us. I held my arm out, and everyone stopped walking.

"Is it the Murk?" asked Teila.

"No, that's an animal."

In seconds, a pack of wild dogs emerged from the trees.

Cameron took a step, and I grabbed his arm. "Do. Not. Run," I stated.

They advanced slowly, each dog putting distance between the next. Their eyes glowed like tiny orbs of fire, their teeth bared.

"They've been guarding this place," said Chana. That's when I realized the twin knew exactly what she was talking about when she mentioned the first dog being a scout.

The pack advanced slowly, circling us. "Nobody panic," I told them. "Any sudden move could make them attack."

"They're going to attack anyway," said Parker. "That's what they're here for."

The largest of the dogs looked as if it had been dipped in water and then its fur froze. It looked back at the other dogs, growled again, and they dashed away from us.

"What just happened? Why didn't they do anything?" asked Justin.

"It knows we're here," said Corey.

I glanced over my shoulder. "Theodore—"

"I know," he replied. "Quincy, Bradly..." They stepped beside him. "Okay, okay," he kept saying while rubbing his hands together.

"Calm down, Theodore."

The fear showed in his eyes. Ariel clasped his hand and his expression softened.

"We have to do this. Now. While I have whatever Ariel just gave me."

The three of them clasped hands for a moment. "Remember," said Theodore. "Whatever it took to bring the Murk in, do it again. I don't hate my father, but I will think about all of those things that gave me those thoughts in the first place and allow the rage to build again, even though I know what's right."

"I'll focus on my step-father," said Quincy. "Those feelings have never changed."

They waited for Bradly's response. "I'm ready," was all she replied.

Theodore led the girls forward. They formed a triangle, pointing in the direction the dogs came from.

We lagged behind, leaving the Trojan horse out front.

TIME REMAINING: 45 MINUTES

CHAPTER 39

THEODORE

B radly, Quincy, and I forged ahead. Our determined strides cut through the eerie stillness as we followed the tracks left by the dogs to a desolate camp. The cabins loomed like ghostly remnants of summers long past—windows shattered and doors hanging off the hinges. Their wooden frames were weather-beaten and worn from years of neglect. We reached what appeared to be the main building, its warped sign barely readable above the entrance: Sector 66.

Did that mean each camp was a sector, so there were sixty-five before this one? Dread washed over me like an icy wave.

I gritted my teeth, forcing myself to look straight ahead and not glance back at the Knights. It might cause me to change my mind. I couldn't, because I had to do this for Sheena. My best friend. The girl I loved. My secret crush. There was no better time to admit it to myself, but I had to focus. *You better not screw this up,* was the last normal thought I had. The darkest memories emerged from the back of my mind, and I grasped at them, allowing them to fill me. Suddenly, I found myself transported back two years, to a time when the Murk had infected me and I hated my father and wanted to harm myself.

I struggled to stay in that place, as we moved deeper into the core of the camp, where the putrid scent of decay lingered in the air.

A deep, primal darkness churned in the pit of my stomach, threatening to consume me. Quincy and Bradly stepped up beside me.

Quincy's gaze hardened. Bradly stared ahead, unflinching. Above us, our breaths hung visible in the frigid air.

We heard it before we saw it. The crackling of energy in the air, and then a guttural moan mixed with thunder.

Ahead of us, a mass of fog grew thicker, obscuring everything from view. It moved toward us and coiled around our bodies, alive.

The Murk's growl of a voice echoed, beckoning us closer with its eerie invitation: "Welcome home...to your final resting place."

We exchanged tense glances.

"You must first prove yourselves worthy," the Murk continued. "Find the courage to face the darkness within."

With its words still hanging in the air, the fog receded from us. *Is it leaving? It can't leave.*

"What now?" Quincy whispered.

Bradly took a deep breath, her shoulders squared. "We do as the Murk says. We let the darkness in."

She was right. There was no turning back now. Nor did I want to, for Sheena's sake. I grasped Bradly and Quincy's hands one last time before focusing on the darkest thoughts possible. The ties to my friends and all others fell away.

The air buzzed with electricity as we followed the fog. It lowered, and I stepped inside the swirling mist.

CHAPTER 40

LOGAN

A low-pitched bark and growling echoed through the clearing.

I stopped walking. "They're back."

The dogs emerged from the thick fog, their breaths billowing in the frigid weather. They stood like sentinels, guarding the entrance to the camp, blocking us off from Theodore, Quincy, and Bradly.

Past the dogs, my friends moved into the heart of the camp, the Murk's current lair. Before them stood a weather-beaten roof-only pole building. There were no walls, and its steep metal covering was partially torn from the frame. Underneath were the remnants of its former purpose—a weathered podium and rusted benches.

I watched Theodore, Quincy, and Bradly step into the fog beyond the building. In seconds, the Murk materialized, its lava-like form barely discernible through the thick, smokey haze. It loomed over the camp and lowered toward the ground. Theodore, Quincy, and Bradly walked right into it.

"They went in," said Justin, as if we couldn't all see it, the shock apparent in his voice.

"How long do you think it will take them to get to her?" asked Jasmine.

"We don't know. We know nothing about what happens inside of it," I replied. For a moment, as I watched the vortex ahead of us, doubt crept in. Was the Trojan horse really a good plan? They'd have to fight off an unfathomable darkness to free themselves and Sheena. Theodore was determined. I knew he would try as hard as he could. Bradly would also. But, there was something about Quincy. Even though she wasn't a Knight of the Gleam, she had a strength and fearlessness about her. Maybe she was the help Theodore and Bradly needed to pull this off.

"Are you afraid of the dark?" The Murk hissed as it spread high above us and its fog blocked out the moon.

We huddled closer together. "Cameron, how much time do we have?" I asked, flashing the light from my phone around us. The Knights followed suit.

"Does it matter at this point?"

His words told all I needed to know. We were almost out of time.

The pack of snarling dogs closed in on us, their teeth bared and hackles raised.

Ariel gasped. "Are they going to attack?"

"They better not try," I replied, moving in front of her, feeling energy flowing to my fingertips.

"Maybe we should back up. If it looks like we're leaving, they may leave us alone," said Parker.

But the dogs surrounded us. More in number than what had first approached.

"Let us help," said one of the twins, as she tried to pull from Corey and Justin.

Justin released her arm, and Corey released the other.

Each of the girls wore one of Aunt Belinda's coats. One of them reached for her hood and pulled it back, revealing her face. "Shine a light on me," she said.

Seren used the flashlight from her phone.

Without hesitation, the twin thrust out her hand towards the dogs, and they fell silent at her command. "Allow us passage," she demanded.

The dogs yelped and obediently parted, cowering to the sides.

"Go!" she told us.

We walked through the narrow path the dogs created, without taking our eyes off them.

"Why are they obeying you?" Teila asked the twin.

"Because we trained them."

I was already cold, but her answer sent a chill down my spine.

"Why did she just help us?" whispered Cameron.

"I don't know," I thought aloud.

"Hurry," one of the twins said.

We cleared the dogs and quickly ran across the grounds and didn't stop until we reached the center of the camp. Ahead of us, the landscape vanished from view, obscured by a swirling vortex of dark smog.

"You should not have come here," said a male voice.

Drake stepped out of the Murk. A lone figure, dressed in black, standing at the base of it.

The twins gasped at seeing their brother. "We did this to him," said one of the girls. The other moaned, and Justin shone the light from his phone across their faces.

"Whoa!" he exclaimed and grabbed them again. The whites of their eyes flashed to red.

"This is so not good," said Parker.

One of the twins tried to pull away from Justin to get to Drake. "It's calling us back."

"But you don't have to listen," said Seren.

"Hold them," said Cameron. "They are our Plan B!"

Drake's head tilted. "Plan? What Plan? Did you come here to die? Is that your plan?"

"We're here for Sheena," I replied, trying to sound braver than I felt. Even though my heart raced, one thing was for sure...I was not leaving without her.

The Murk let out a low, rumbling laugh, and Drake extended his arms to the sides. "You cannot defeat me. I am too powerful."

"We'll see about that," I said, taking a step forward. "Stay here," I told everyone else.

"No, don't go," said Chana.

"What are you doing? That wasn't the plan," said Cameron.

"Somebody stop him," said Justin.

As I moved, the mist began to part around me, almost as if it were afraid to touch me. A faint hum filled the air as power flowed through me.

I looked over at the others and saw that they were also glowing faintly. I knew then that we had a chance at taking this thing down.

"We are the Knights of the Gleam," I shouted. The rest of the team joined in. "The force that binds us is God's might. We stand together united; the power of our will is the angel's light. We go forth as His servants to fight for His glory. Let none fall. We conquer in the name of the Lord."

I ran forward, away from my team.

Drake disappeared into thin air, and the Murk let out an enraged roar and flowed around me like a tornado of fire.

Suddenly, a female's blood-curdling scream echoed from everywhere, followed by a sickening crunch. I ran towards the sound, and I saw her. Sheena was lying on the ground, blood pooling around her head. Phoenix stood over her, a sick grin on his face.

"No!" I screamed. It was my worst nightmare. Sheena was gone. We were too late, and I was the one who trusted Phoenix—the one who had defended him countless times—believing that he was more than what the Murk had done to him.

"Phoenix, what have you done?" I yelled.

"What does it look like?" Phoenix sneered. "And now it's your turn."

Phoenix's nostrils flared as he lunged towards me, his eyes filled with a dark, burning hatred. His fists swung wildly, fueled by whatever the Murk had promised him. But I wasn't going to let him win. With every ounce of strength I had, I fought back, forgetting about the Murk. My focus was solely on defending myself against Phoenix's relentless attack. Then Phoenix's fist connected with my jaw, sending me reeling.

"Logan!" I heard the Knights' voices calling. They were near.

Suddenly, Corey was beside me, holding me. "No! Stop! Stop it! Listen to me! Whatever you saw was an illusion. It wasn't real. The Murk uses illusions to get to us. You know this."

I blinked hard and looked around. There was no Phoenix and no Sheena. My hand was throbbing from where I must have hit the ground.

"But I felt him hit me."

"You felt yourself," said Uncle Jonas, clenching my fists. He released them and held one where I could see the bruising.

"How did you get here?" I asked him.

"I have my ways. Looks like I arrived just in time."

Ahead of us, the Murk churned, mocking us. But from somewhere inside it, Quincy's voice yelled. "Now!"

CHAPTER 41

SHEENA

There was no strength left in me. Any hope I had of making it back to my family was depleted. Soon I would be in heaven, and Chana would be there waiting for me on the other side.

At least the Murk wouldn't get what it wanted. Maybe Dingy and my friends would destroy it one day. Hopefully, Dingy would be smarter than me and not haul off trying to do things by himself. He was so young that he could learn early on that gleamers were meant to work together and not end up like me.

Pain. Agony. Torture. They were my constant companions. If this was what hell was like, I wanted no part of it. My desperate cries for Draven went unanswered, leaving me to face the fiery abyss alone. My final thoughts were all over the place, but settled on my mom. All I wanted to do was tell her how much I loved her. The tears streaming down my face quickly turned to steam, as I prayed she knew just how much before the flames consumed me completely.

"Welcome home." The Murk's voice echoed. But who was it talking to?

My eyes closed, succumbing to the torment.

I drifted away again, and when I came too, I could feel...something was wrong. There was less pain, and I could see the night sky and stars above me.

I squeezed my eyes shut. *Either I'm dreaming or this is an illusion. Either way, it doesn't matter. It's too late.* Then, I heard shouting and the sound of firecrackers, and the Murk howling. I forced myself to open my eyes, peering through a smoky haze.

Suddenly I heard Chana's voice. "Hold on, Sheena!"

In another glimpse, there was a clearing of smoke and I saw that Seren and Logan had worked together to create an opening. My father fought around them with... Corey? *He must have revealed his gift to Cameron.*

Even if they could fight the Murk off, the chances of them even finding me were slim. The Murk would probably kill them first.

Either it was their presence or the weakening of the Murk, but moments later I felt stronger, although not myself. My body began to rise, as the invisible chains holding me loosened.

"Where are you going?" Phoenix appeared out of nowhere and grabbed me, just as Luke had done when he found me in that apartment building years ago. He had slammed me against the wall in front of the mural he had painted of me. Phoenix told me how I had haunted his dreams, using the exact words Luke had. It was almost as if they were the same person. The whites of his eyes were red and fluctuating to white.

He's fighting it!

When they were fully white, he pulled me into a hug. "You're not alone," he said. Then he pulled back and shoved me as hard as he could. "Quincy told me to tell you, 'I save you, God saves me!'" he yelled as I tumbled away from him.

I screamed as I flew through the void.

Suddenly, scorching arms caught and wrapped around me. "Where do you think you're going, Sheena Meyer?" asked Drake. "You can't leave this place."

Immediately, Phoenix appeared again. The two fought, and this time, Drake was sent flying through the Murk.

Phoenix grabbed me again. His eyes flashing back and forth, as he placed a hand on either side of my head and brought his face close to mine, as if he might kiss me. "Do what you were created to do," he whispered. "Use the key."

"I'm not strong enough. I'm dying." At least part of me was. The part that made me, me. The Murk was winning—getting what it always wanted.

"Sheena, if you don't do this, it's going to kill your friends. Take my hand," Phoenix said. His hand ran down my arm and found mine. At that moment, I saw the carving from the archeological site. We were both descendants of the boy, Phillip. It wasn't Logan or Dingy that this task was meant for, It was me and Phoenix.

He placed something against my palm. "Logan told me to give this to you when I found you. He said you would know what to do with it."

I opened my hand. *They found the key?*

"He's coming," Phoenix said, looking behind him. "Use the key."

I didn't know which "he" it was, and I couldn't tell if Phoenix was just warning me or was concerned.

Use the key, I told myself. I closed my eyes trying to focus on what was inside me. *We're together. Work key!*

Phoenix shook me. "Wake up, Sheena. Use the key!"

Before he could say anything further, Marcus grabbed him. Phoenix fought him off, and Marcus lunged toward me. *Fight, Sheena*, I screamed in my head. With one hand, I grabbed his face. With the other, I wielded the key like a makeshift weapon, aiming for his eye. He recoiled with a howl of pain, but quickly recovered, advancing quickly. Before he could get to me, Phoenix cut him off and the two fought again.

"Draven," I screamed. "I know you can hear me. Help us!"

"Sheena!"

Wait, I know that voice. "Teddy?" *It can't be.*

"Sheena!" It called again.

"I'm here!"

Quincy, Teddy, and Bradly came out of nowhere. Draven was with them.

"We came to get you out of here. The Murk had us, but Draven freed us," said Teddy.

"Help Phoenix!" I exclaimed. It was no time for details.

They all flew at Marcus, weightless, suspended within the Murk's swirling vortex. I didn't know how it was possible they were inside the Murk with me, but the three of them glowed as they attacked Marcus from every angle. A blue energy emanating from Phoenix and Draven cast dramatic shafts of light around them.

This is it! It's happening. The key...no, something was wrong. I clasped the key tightly in my hand and closed my eyes willing it to work, but nothing happened. Phoenix and I were here—the two figures on the drawing. But with or without this key, it wasn't working.

At first, I thought the key was the hope that engulfed me—that was growing and strengthening in me as we fought together toward our goal. But then there was this ornate key in my hand with Marcus's blood dripping from it. What was I missing? There had to be something more, some final piece to activate its power.

The Murk was weakening. I could see outside of its smokey nebulous, as it lowered to the ground. I repeatedly tried to summon some type of power within me, but nothing happened.

Chana, where are you? I thought.

In a glimpse, too quick to know if I had really seen them in the spirit realm, angels fought along with Chana's guardian form against the Murk. And in that realm, the Murk looked nothing like it did on Earth. It was almost embarrassing that this was what we feared. Something shrouded by a dark cloud.

"Remember the journal," came Draven's voice.

The journal... My mind flashed to the words I read: *if you throw something, such as a wire, over two of these power lines, it will be in contact with two phases, or phase to phase. This is dangerous because the voltage between two phases is much higher than the voltage between one phase and the neutral line. If a wire comes into contact with two phases, it can cause a short circuit, which can result in an explosion, meaning serious damage.*

Short circuit? Wait a minute...

"I understand!" I screamed.

It was me! I had to bring about that short circuit.

I squeezed my eyes shut, but again, nothing happened. I started to panic. If I didn't do something soon, the Murk would have us all. I couldn't let that happen, but I didn't know what to do. So for a moment, I let go. I allowed the Murk's force to slash against me like a thousand knives and... I prayed for help. Right there in the midst of the battle, as if nothing else mattered. I had to get to the source of our gleam.

"Well done..." My eyes flashed open, hearing Nana's voice.

The ground trembled violently, revealing a gaping hole directly beneath the Murk. The City of Gleamers descendants formed a circle around the hole, their hands pulsating with a force that held the Murk down, preventing it from escaping into the sky.

Then I saw her. "No, no, no..." I muttered.

My mother climbed from the roof of a pole building and threw herself inside the Murk.

"No!" I screamed.

At the same time, I dropped the key and the vision of the archaeological site flashed vividly in my mind once more: Two identical stick people holding hands, one larger than the other, and a bolt of lightning between them.

Through the Murk's chaotic current, my mother screamed for me.

Realization struck me. My eyes widened. *My mom?* It was always us. Me and my mother. But how?

Only one explanation could make sense of it all.

She's a gleamer...just like me.

And that bolt of lightning—the key—was our love.

I stretched forward and caught my mother as she came through the Murk's churning tendrils of fog. The feel of her touch, her embrace, her strength...took my breath away. She held me tight.

"Now, Sheena!" said Chana.

I looked up through an opening in the weakened smoke. The guardians had stopped fighting. They were watching. This wasn't for them to do. It was for me and my mom. Their only job was to weaken it.

Without thinking, I had taken my eyes off of what they were supposed to be on. My mother cried out as she was pried away from me. In a flash, Draven and Phoenix grabbed her and sent her flying back toward me. I reached out, grabbing her arm and pulling her in with all my might.

With a primal scream, I summoned the dormant power within me. Energy surged through my body pulsing with an intensity that I had never felt before. The same glowed from within my mother, illuminating her.

"No!" Marcus screamed.

The world around us shook and trembled as the key unlocked a force that exploded from within us. A surge so intense that it manifested as a blinding flash of white light that consumed everything around me. Intense heat surrounded us, accompanied by a popping sound I couldn't explain.

From where we were, in the sky, I could see the lights of a town. Behind us, an electrical arc connected with a nearby power line. The city lights in the distance went out.

The Murk tried to lift off, but somehow, my friends and the City of Gleamers held it there. It lowered until I held my mom with one hand and I reached and grabbed onto a power line with the other. We became a conduit, and I watched as the arc, like a large white fireball, surged along the wire, coming right for us.

I didn't know what would happen when it reached us. This could be the end—for all of us. My mom's hand squeezed mine, and though there had been no words between us, we were in agreement. We clung to each other, and I clung to the wire, watching the arc's approach.

I looked into her eyes. "I love you, Mommy."

TIME REMAINING: 10 SECONDS

CHAPTER 42

SHEENA

The explosion blinded me, as the wire in my hand went slack. My mother and I still held each other tightly, as overbearing screeching, screams, and cries came from all around us. The air crackled with residual energy and filled with the scent of ozone.

With trembling hands, I released my grip on the power line.

The Murk recoiled, its tentacles writhing in agony. Its grip on me slackened, and I seized the opportunity. With all the strength I could muster, I tore myself free, ripping through what was left of its lava-like walls with ease. And pulling my mother along with me, I emerged from the Murk, panting and sweating.

And so did Draven, his hands on his knees, panting.

Logan grabbed Phoenix in a hug, and Corey grabbed them both.

Teddy, Quincy, and Bradly held to each other with huge grins. "Can't tell me, I'm not a gleamer too," said Quincy.

Ariel and Seren ran to me. Then Chana appeared. "You never left me," I whispered, as she hugged me.

My dad landed in front of us as if it was normal for people to float in the air.

"Is it dead?" asked Parker, wiping the ash from his face, and glancing around at the cabins that were on fire.

We watched the Murk recoil and shrink down to the size of an exercise ball. Smoke and char, blood and lava. It was a disgusting mess that turned inside itself and disappeared.

"I think what was left of Marcus after the explosion may have been mixed up in that."

"Gross," said Teila.

Everyone gathered around me. I couldn't stop the tears. My mother held me up with a strength I didn't know she had. Any amount of energy I once had, had gone into creating that arc of electricity and pulling us out of the Murk. I would have collapsed if it weren't for her.

"Where is Nana?"

"At home being a super hostess with the rest of the City of Gleamers descendants," said Chana.

"But I saw them— Never mind."

Draven stood far off from everyone else, seeing to his sisters. I motioned to him. The group parted and let him inside our circle. "Thank you," he told me. "I knew you could do it."

"Not without you," I replied. My throat was like sandpaper and sore.

"Let's get you home," my mother said.

Parker pointed at the back of Bodhi's head. "Woah."

Bodhi's hair lifted away from his collar, as if from static electricity.

"I think there's something behind us," said Jasmine.

We all turned.

The angel boy appeared. The same boy we had chased out of Muskegon High School to that park. He backed away. "Knights of the Gleam," he trumpeted, although his mouth didn't move.

My mother slowly let go of me with her arms extended, making sure I could stand on my own. My father and Chana were on either side of her. I wobbled and Cameron caught me. "I've got you, Angel Girl."

We followed the boy back several feet.

The boy motioned, and Draven, Seren, and Quincy followed as well. Then he pointed at Logan. Logan looked down and patted his pocket. He reached inside and removed a small vial. The boy nodded.

"What's that?" I asked.

"Nana's anointing oil," said Ariel.

The boy tapped above his nose. "Oh," said Logan. He uncapped the oil and walked around the group, placing a dab on each of our foreheads.

The boy transformed, standing ten-feet taller, and gazed upon me and my friends with a radiant glow, his wings outspread in majestic splendor. He spoke with a voice that echoed with both power and grace. "Knights of the Gleam, champions of light, you have triumphed over the forces of darkness and extinguished the entity that threatened to shroud this world in eternal despair. Your valor and unity have proven that the power of hope and righteousness can overcome even the deepest abyss.

"You are the Knights of the Gleam, chosen to safeguard the light that resides within every heart. The battle you fought was not just against a tangible foe, but a testament to the indomitable spirit that resides within each of you.

"As you stand here victorious, know that your actions ripple through the tapestry of existence, weaving threads of hope and courage. The world, once threatened by the encroaching darkness, now basks in the warmth of your deeds. The Gleam that emanates from your very souls illuminates the path toward a brighter tomorrow.

"Yet the journey does not end here. Your purpose extends beyond this battlefield. May the gleam guide your steps as you venture forth, and may your hearts remain steadfast in the face of challenges that arise. Remember, as Knights of the Gleam, you are bound by a sacred duty—to nurture hope, protect the innocent, and ensure that the brilliance of the gleam prevails.

"Go forth, champions. This, beloved Knights, is your legacy. You are the Knights of the gleam. The force that binds us is God's might. You stand together united; the power of your will is the angel's light. Go forth as His servants to fight for His glory. Let none fall. Conquer in the name of the Lord."

The angel disappeared in a flash of light.

When I glanced around at my friends, the gleam shone from each of their eyes. Piercing and expanding in and out. Stronger than I had ever seen it.

"Sheena?" they began saying one by one. Everyone looked at me with wide eyes.

Bradly grinned.

I didn't know why, but I felt stronger now—like myself again. I looked at my hands. They weren't cracked and gray like twins when I pulled them out. I glanced at Draven. He looked normal, too.

"What is it?"

"Your hair," said Ariel.

I grabbed at it, thinking the Murk might have fried it off. I was relieved to feel a handful of curls, and pulled one toward my face. "My-my hair is brown again."

Everyone grinned, but no words were spoken. And we all came in for a group hug, except for Draven.

"You're one of us, now," said Corey.

He stepped closer. "And what does that mean?"

"You're redeemed."

"And Phoenix..." said Bradly.
He turned to her.
"You're atoned."

CHAPTER 43

SHEENA

A flicker of hope ignited in Draven's eyes, and he acknowledged his newfound redemption with a teary nod. Phoenix, too, rubbed the tears from his eyes.

The Knights of the Gleam clasped hands. I could feel the strength in our bond intensify as we stood there, connected not only by our mission but by our shared understanding and forgiveness.

"I think it's time to go home," said Corey. "Someone is bound to see these cabins on fire out here."

Quincy backed away, grabbed a board from the ground, and thrust it into the flames, watching as it quickly caught fire. She then turned and began setting every surface she could find ablaze

Justin grabbed her. "Really? After you were just knighted with us. What are you doing?"

"Let it all burn," she replied.

I couldn't disagree.

"That's enough," my father said, as he took the board from her and hurled it into the fire of one of the cabins.

The group dismantled, and my eyes met Logan's. As the leader of the Knights, I knew he had been instrumental in making all of this happen. "Thank you, Co-bro," I mouthed. We grinned at each other as Chana embraced me in a hug, followed by Ariel.

"You know, I knew you and Phoenix had something planned all along," Teddy told Logan.

"Sure you did."

My father waited, alone, as the others went to help my mom with the twins.

"Lucy, you've got some explaining to do," I said, mimicking Ricky Ricardo. My dad and I had watched that 50s show together for years on a streaming service.

He gave a slight smirk before lifting me off my feet in a hug.

"Daddy, it's okay. It's okay," I repeated. I couldn't tell if he was crying, but he wouldn't let go. Not until my mother came over.

"Jonas..." was all she said. He put me down and turned away.

"This was really hard on him."

I nodded, tears filling my eyes.

"Hey, what was the 'Plan B' I heard someone mention?"

"I didn't hear all of it," my mom replied, "but something about leaving Dingy with the twins, and his being in danger causing you to burst out of the Murk."

I thought for a moment. "That doesn't sound right."

She shrugged. "They've had smarter ideas. Let's go." She took my hand as we followed the others across the field. Every once in a while, Teddy or Cameron looked back at us. I didn't know if it was to make sure I was still okay, or because it was hard to believe I was really free.

"So...When were you going to tell me you were a gleamer?" I asked my mom.

She sighed. "Never. It would only reveal the likelihood of you being who you are."

I frowned, confused.

She turned to face me briefly with a smirk on her face before turning forward again.

"How do you gleam?" I pressed on, hoping for some answers.

"Wouldn't you like to know?" she teased, giving me a playful nudge with her shoulder.

I chuckled and shook my head. There were always secrets. But that was okay. I was just glad to be alive and free, with my mom by my side.

CHAPTER 44

LOGAN

*F*our hours later

I jolted awake and sat up. For a moment, I didn't know where I was or what day it was. The room was a symphony of snores. They came at different pitches, with a few whistles, and a couple of snorts from Justin.

No one had left Sheena's house after our return. I didn't know if they all felt safer there or if no one was ready to part ways after her being home.

We had all taken showers, with the boys borrowing clothes from me and Uncle Jonas. It was a struggle to find something large enough for Justin, though. The girls dressed in Sheena's clothes, and as the sun started to rise, each of us found a spot in the house to rest and eventually dozed off, parents included.

Across the room, near the fireplace, I spotted Ariel snuggled up next to her father.

I stood up, carefully stepped over Phoenix, and walked through the family room, dining room, and living room, around the bodies snoring on pillows or wrapped in blankets. Beyond the living room, I walked into the sunroom and stood there watching snowflakes drift past the window.

We did it. We really did it.

Soft footsteps came from behind me, and I turned to see Sheena padding quietly into the room. We exchanged weary grins, but didn't speak. I simply took her hand in mine, gave it a gentle squeeze, and together we watched the snow fall.

"You know," she whispered after a few minutes, breaking our comfortable silence, "towards the end there, I really thought I was going to die."

A pang of guilt hit me.

"Don't do that," Sheena scolded me. "I see that frown. None of this was your fault. I planned to go inside the Murk to save Draven. There was nothing anyone could have done to stop me. Where is he anyway?"

I pointed at him in a corner with an arm around each of his sisters, asleep. For a moment, I wondered: *If I had been through all that they had, could I sleep? Would I have nightmares?*

Uncle Jonas sat on the floor near them. He didn't fool me. His eyes were closed with his arms folded over his chest, but I doubted he was asleep. He would stay in protector gleamer mode until the Hues' were back with their parents.

"That's not okay," I said, pointing at Sheena's feet in two different fuzzy socks.

She chuckled softly and rubbed the back of her neck. "Yeah, well you know me, Co-bro."

"You know, I think I might," I said and draped an arm over her shoulders. We stayed like that for a while until we heard someone behind us. We pulled away from each other to see Ariel standing there with a smile on her face.

She clasped her hands together. "You really see each other now. You're going to need that for what's to come."

"Wait, what?"

"Just joking," she replied with a wink and walked away.

I turned to Sheena. "Is she joking?"

"Don't ask me. She's *your* girlfriend."

CHAPTER 45

SHEENA

*O*ne Month Later

I was beginning to think that it would be impossible to recapture what I'd lost before finding out I was a gleamer—to feel normal again—but I was wrong.

As soon as I stepped outside my house, raindrops landed on my skin, like a soft caress from heaven above. They made a light tapping noise on the umbrella as I opened it. I smiled, breathing in the fresh air.

I walked toward the backyard and thought back on my childhood, on the lessons that I had learned since then and the wisdom that Nana had imparted to me. I remembered how she would talk about angels and how they were always watching and guiding us. As I thought about it, I looked up at the family room window. My mother stood there watching me. I smiled at her, and she blew me a kiss.

I thought *I* had held the biggest secret, that I wasn't the Angelus Bellator—but it was my mother who held the biggest secret. She explained that in order to hide the Angelus Bellator and his protector, no one could know about her. It would take two gleamers to create me. This threw the Murk off for years, but still it kept watch because of Nana being such a powerful gleamer and it knew of the Tobias bloodline, which we were part of. But next door was the real Angelus Bellator, and the Murk had no idea.

I think the most amazing part of it all was the secret plan that Logan and Phoenix had. Phoenix allowed the Murk to take him so that when the time was right, he could fight it off and help me—and give me the key. A key that Nana informed us was fake. The whole "key" mystery was about throwing the Murk off and keeping it from discovering what the true key was.

But just as incredible as Logan and Phoenix's plan was how Bradly, Teddy, and Quincy allowed it to reinfect them so they could get inside.

All of them endured so much for me, but also to save all kids from the Murk.

As I glanced back at my willow tree watching rain drop through its branches, I let the umbrella fall to my side and lifted my face, feeling alive—free. Suddenly, I felt hands grasp my shoulders. I looked back at my mother. Her hand clasped mine, and we laughed and danced in the spring rain as my father and Nana watched approvingly from the window, their smiles mirroring the unspoken understanding that our journey had come full circle.

We twirled and spun, our laughter floating through the air as the rain soaked our clothes. In that shared dance, I found a sense of renewal. The willow tree, a silent witness to our celebration, stood like a sentinel guarding our newfound peace.

And so, beneath the spring rain, surrounded by the love of my family, I embraced the beauty of the moment. The secret plan, the hidden thorns, and all the sacrifices made had gotten us to this place of peace.

The story of the Angelus Bellator was far from over, but the echoes of its lessons would forever resonate in the hearts of those who had dared to challenge the darkness.

A new story was forming—one of courage, unity, and unwavering determination. The Knights of the Gleam, bound by a shared destiny and fueled by the power of love, stood ready to face whatever challenges lay ahead. With my family by my side, I knew that together, we would write the next chapter in the gleamer legacy.

As we danced, an ethereal glow enveloped us, illuminating the raindrops as if a myriad of tiny stars had descended upon our backyard. It was as if the angels themselves were watching over us, their presence palpable in every drop that caressed our skin.

My parents, Nana, Chana, Logan, Phoenix, Teddy, Corey, Cameron, Quincy, Ariel, Seren—all of the team—they had each risked so much on this journey. I wondered what was next for the Knights of the Gleam.

But for now, those thoughts faded into the background. The rain continued to fall around us as we twirled and laughed, my long brown curls soaked into waves.

Suddenly, my mother stopped dancing and looked up at the sky with a smile on her face. "Do you see that?" she asked excitedly.

I followed her gaze and saw a beautiful rainbow stretching across the sky as the sun began to peek out from behind gray clouds.

We watched in awe as the sky brightened around the rainbow, a symbol of hope and promise. The rain became a light mist, washing away the remnants of the past. I looked forward to the future with hope and anticipation. For in the end, it was the light that we carried within our hearts that defined us. And with that light as our guide, there was nothing we could not overcome.

"The most beautiful word on the lips of mankind is the word 'Mother,' and the most beautiful call is the call of "My mother." It is a word full of hope and love, a sweet and kind word coming from the depths of the heart. The mother is everything—she is our consolation in sorrow, our hope in misery, and our strength in weakness. She is the source of love, mercy, sympathy, and forgiveness...."

~KAHLIL GIBRAN

PLEASE LEAVE A REVIEW

Your review means the world to me. I greatly appreciate any kind words.
Even one or two sentences go a long way in helping readers discover Angel Girl Awakening.
Thank you in advance.

Don't Miss Out!
Sign up to be of the first informed when Knights of the Gleam Book 3 releases. Expect *Sacrifice of Echoes* in 2025
Exclusive content, discounts, and giveaways are available only to L. B. Anne's VIP members.
There is no charge or obligation.
www.lbanne.com/vip-club

Have you read L. B. Anne's Everfall series?
It's another series in the Sheena Meyer Universe

Before I Let Go
What if you were sent back in time to save your own life?
An angel has transported Aria back to the year 1982, the year her family moved to Michigan.
She'd turned fourteen, was obsessed with E.T, and spent every afternoon glued to the television watching MTV. It was also the year she made a list of all the terrible things done to her and the people who betrayed her.
Aria's life hangs in the balance as she relives the bullying and humiliation that led to a terrible decision. Guided by an angel, she must change her past or deal with the consequences of giving up... again.
Fighting through the same severe depression and anxiety that ailed her so many years ago, Aria learns why her life is worth living.
A story of faith, forgiveness, strength, love, and redemption.

Read an excerpt of
Never Really Gone
Meet Gabbie and Micah.
never really gone
L.B. ANNE

NEVER REALLY GONE

I can't sleep.

As soon as I close my eyes, I'm back at Micah's funeral. To be honest, I don't even want to try to sleep anymore.

Instead, I look to the right of my bed at Micah's unfinished watercolor mural and remember every bit of the most painful day of my life; the heat in the sanctuary making the perfumes of those around me overpowering, the sniffles and cries, even my own. All of it, so vivid.

I remember thinking, *does it always rain during funerals?* I'd thought that was just a movie cliche to make scenes more forlorn or dramatic, but there was a storm that day. Not while we were tucked inside of Mount Hope Church fanning ourselves. The air conditioning had been out for days, and the sanctuary was so packed with people I was sure we broke the capacity fire code.

I wiped beads of sweat from my forehead. A stream trickled down my neck, disappearing into the ruffled collar of my blouse.

My mother's shoulder pressed into mine. "Are you okay?" she asked.

I pulled the neckline of my shirt away from my sticky skin and rubbed the sweat on my skirt. "Yeah. It's so hot in here."

"It shouldn't be much longer," she said and patted my lap.

The organist's fingers glided over the keys as he played the intro of the next hymn. At least the thrumming of rain would have flooded out Mother Beck's off-key rendition of "His Eye is on the Sparrow."

The wall of stained glass behind her, which usually emanated rays of color, looked dull that day. A choir stood below the massive cross at the center of the wall. They struggled through the hymn. Some members were too overcome to sing, their sweat and tears tinted with makeup and dripping onto their white robes. You had to know Micah to understand. Everyone loved him. He was a magnet for goodness and generosity. When he was around, something good was sure to happen. For instance, a car in front of us paying for our order at the Starbucks drive-thru. Or the time this guy was like, "He kid, here's two tickets to the New York Knicks game tonight. I can't go. You can have them."

At first, I thought things like that happened for no reason at all, but that's not true. It happened to good people, and I benefited because of my proximity to a good person.

How did I get so lucky to have Micah as a boyfriend? Me. With all of my issues. He worked so hard to save me from myself, and now he's the one that's gone. I didn't understand it.

My toes ached from my pointed shoes, and I tugged at the heel, trying to slide my foot out some.

"Stop fidgeting," my mother had whispered. The black veil hanging from her hat grazed my freshly silk-pressed hair, now curling at the roots because of my sweating.

I wished I'd worn a hat with a veil also. And earplugs. And dark glasses.

Watching Micah's mother collapse over his casket in tortured sobs and listening to the wails from those around me had only heightened my emotions.

Many of the mourners lined up to pay their last respects at the casket. Some, still soaked in disbelief, shook their heads and asked, "Why?"

The line moved quickly. My mother joined them, but I didn't. I couldn't move. Soon, I was the only one still sitting on the second-row pew, my eyes lowered, listening.

The body in that casket was not my Micah, and I refused to allow it to become an image embedded in my memory, so I didn't look.

To prepare myself for the funeral, I'd done some research. The part that stuck with me was a rare occurrence, and it was just my luck it would happen. Once a body is placed in a sealed casket, the gases from decomposing can't escape anymore. The pressure increases and the casket becomes like an overblown balloon. It doesn't explode like one, but it can spill out unpleasant fluids and gases. At the thought of it, my stomach twisted, and I grasped it, feeling I might puke.

Breathe, I told myself as I waited for my mother to return and silently prayed Micah wouldn't explode.

Next was the burial. We rode in the limo with Micah's family. His mother insisted on it.

Once we pulled out of the church parking lot, Micah's uncle loosened his tie. "It was a beautiful homegoing service, wasn't it?"

"Yes, it was," my mother replied and squeezed my hand. I was glad she was there to answer because I couldn't. I watched Micah's little brother lean against his mother's bosom and stare at his black patent leather shoes he'd been kicking off the entire day. He didn't make a sound, only looked at his shoes, hardly blinking.

I flipped over the funeral program on my lap. Micah's face smiled up at me from his sophomore year photo as I prepared myself for the worst part of the day—the final goodbye.

The funeral procession led across town to Beacon Cemetery. We entered through a pair of tall white stone pillars and a wrought iron gate, then followed a never-ending road that wound around the burial sections.

We passed beds of chrysanthemums boasting blooms in a kaleidoscope of colors, along with smaller sections of ornamental cabbage plants. I had a passion for flowers and plants. There were few I didn't know. And if I was lucky enough to go to college—meaning, if my family could afford it—I'd become a botanist and own my own nursery one day. For now, I was satisfied with working part-time at the flower shop around the corner from my house.

The limo came to a stop, followed by more cars than I could count. Six pallbearers—Chase, Micah's older brother, two cousins, and two uncles—carried the casket from the hearse to the grave.

My mother and I followed Micah's family across the lawn to Micah's burial plot.

For a moment, I couldn't breathe. Then my mother's hand grazed my back and she pressed me close to her.

Everyone stood in black suits and dresses around the grave where a mahogany casket covered in an ornate display of white orchids, dahlias, and roses was ready to be lowered into the ground. The smell of fresh cut grass was strong, and it mingled with the scent of Micah's uncle's aftershave beside me.

Chase wore an oversized black raincoat over a black suit. His face was red from crying.

I looked over at him and caught his eye. He gave me a weak smile. I gave him a look that said, I am here. He nodded as if to say, I know.

The sun had shone for a moment when we left Mount Hope Church. But by the time we arrived at the cemetery, the skies were dark and angry. The wind howled. Thunder clapped. Lightning flashed. It was as if God himself was trying to tell me something.

The funeral director milled around like she was looking for someone, but the lenses of her round glasses were so dark, I was sure she was doing her best not to witness our pain. Maybe she'd known Micah too. By the look of the crowd, the entire city had.

I watched with my head on my mother's shoulder. And just before the casket lowered, I wondered, Is Micah really in there? Maybe all the graves in the cemetery were really empty.

I know. It was an odd thought to have while the minister prayed.

Droplets of rain landed on the casket. One at a time as if someone were dropping them from a single eye dropper. And then, many eye droppers. A torrential downpour.

Black umbrellas popped open here and there, but most didn't seem to mind the weather. It was the least of my worries. Someone sang a hymn, and then a couple of people approached the podium to say a few words. When they finished, the pastor asked for a moment of silence, during which Micah's mother burst into screams. Several people unsuccessfully tried to console her as the casket was lowered into the ground.

I knew exactly how she felt—how each and every person who'd lost someone felt. I knew, because I felt the same way. The same pain. I just had a different way of showing it. There was a dark room inside me that I disappeared into and shut the door. It helped me deal with the numbness and kept me from having to respond to the pain or even eat.

In the end, I was the last person standing at the grave. Soaked and shivering, still looking down at Micah's casket, waiting. But waiting for what?

A lone figure stood several feet away. The only person not dressed in black, he wore a gray hoodie and torn jeans. He waved and walked away.

As I watched the stranger leave, a hand touched my shoulder. "It's time to go, Brie," my mother said, her voice filled with sorrow and pity. She'd gone to get her umbrella from the limo and now held it over me.

I glanced at her, and then down at the grave, then once more at the headstone before I walked away.

In Loving Memory
Micah George
2006-2022

That day, if you had asked me what I thought happened to Micah or anyone after they died, I would've told you I was certain Micah was looking down at us from heaven. That he was shaking his head at us because we took this place a little too seriously. That I'd never see him again.

But today...

I'd tell you we are never really gone.

The Night of the Funeral

As far as I was concerned, Micah's death was only true while I was at the funeral. At home, alone, I wouldn't allow myself to believe he was gone. That's when I missed him most and expected him to call or text. I wanted to hear his voice, and one of his stories—even if they were far-fetched—and his always-think-positive attitude which usually annoyed the heck out of me.

I replayed his voicemails just to hear the sound of his voice. It cracked in the older ones and deepened in the more recent. I read his texts to myself frequently and studied the way he'd written the messages. He never used emojis. Ever. So I used as many as I could for him to interpret or just to frustrate him. But Micah loved GIFs, and he used the same ones over and over as if they were the only five or six available in the world. His favorites were of a toddler dancing or pumping his fist in the air and some comedian I didn't know making a face.

I missed Micah so much. I wanted to see him squint at me with annoyance like he did when I had made an argument that made little sense and hear his laugh when my jokes were not funny.

It was two years after the pandemic. We were back in school and happy about seeing each other every day again in person rather than by Zoom, Facetime, Skype, or Meta Portal. We thought we were safe.

No one knew about Micah's heart condition. We found out when he came down with the virus. It happened so fast. One day, he was healthy and laughing his head off into his face mask as I attempted to piggyback him down the hall to the gym. The next thing I knew, he was fighting for his life, unable to breathe without a ventilator.

I never knew if Micah was aware of the hours I sat waiting in the hospital for him to open his eyes. Or if he could feel me holding his hand all those days. I wanted him to see me there and smile. I planned to tell him to get better and that we still had to terrorize Elle and Chase. I wanted to tell him that we had more pranks to pull on our parents and how excited I was about our plans for winter break. Most of all, I wanted to tell him that I loved him—something I'd never been able to say.

But I never got to.

After a few weeks of him being in the hospital, Micah's mother and the school security officer pulled me out of class.

"Micah is awake," she said. "Come with me." Her words, spoken with a slight Caribbean accent, held no sorrow, nor did they hold the happiness I would've expected. She said nothing further and being quiet was not something Mrs. George was known for.

I hurried after her while my mother signed me out at the office. I had no idea that Micah's parents had made the decision—the most difficult choice they had ever had to make. They were transporting Micah to a hospice.

"Okay," I said. Just like that. Like no big deal. I thought it was a rehab center. I'm a teenager, how would I know what a hospice was and that they were taking him there to...

I remember my parents' faces. They had come to console me, I knew. I didn't react right then. Instead, I tried to be strong for Micah's parents. But inside, I screamed. I screamed for Micah not to go.

My mother always says, "You have to stay prayed up, because you never know what may happen, and you won't have the time to ask for forgiveness for your sins." She wasn't a religious fanatic or anything. There were just some things that were non-negotiable. One was her faith. The other was prayer. But her words did cross my mind in those last moments. Had Micah had a chance to pray before his heart gave out? Or did it happen in an instant—gone from breathing on his own without a mask and tube to standing in front of the pearly gates?

The hours after Micah's passing were the most painful time of my life. They turned to days with me barely noticing time passing. I got tired of everyone constantly asking me if I was okay. I wanted to respond with, "Are you? Imagine if you were fifteen and your sixteen-year-old boyfriend died. Would you be okay?" I don't know why people ask when they know you're not. You can be there for someone without asking that or even speaking.

No matter how much I tried to fake it, I wasn't okay. And it wasn't just about losing my best friend. Or that I missed him so much I thought my heart would explode. Something else was happening.

I'd just gotten out of the shower. I grabbed my robe from the hook on the door, slipped into it, and then switched on my blow dryer. The cool air quickly cleared the steam from the mirror. I stood for a long time, staring at my reflection, my long wavy hair dripping over my back. My swollen eyelids. I didn't know what I was looking for. I felt empty. Maybe I was looking for the Gabriella that was strong enough to get through the coming days without Micah.

I sighed, scrunched a towel through my strands, and shook my hair.

That's when I saw him.

Micah's image materialized in the mirror beside mine.

"Micah?" I gasped and dropped the towel. My hand flew up, covering my open mouth.

Wait. Don't cue the ominous music. It wasn't spooky. Micah didn't float in like a ghost or suddenly appear with a flash of light. It was a gentle entrance.

He wasn't smiling, but he looked peaceful. I blinked, then looked away from the mirror and to my right, expecting to find him standing there. But he wasn't. When I returned my gaze to the mirror, his image was gone, replaced by the reflection of my bedroom behind me.

I continued to stare into the mirror, not quite sure what to make of the image I had just seen.

My heart sank. I covered my face with my hands and whined into them with short breaths before resting them on the sink. I stared at the chipped black polish on my fingernails and then back at the mirror at my red eyes, certain I was having some kind of psychotic break. I shook my head and turned away trying to push the image of Micah out of my mind.

I switched off the bathroom light, climbed in bed with my wet hair, and curled into a ball on my side. I prayed and had high hopes that sleep would find me. But I guess God wasn't in the mood to answer prayers. At least not that night.

When it was obvious I wasn't going to sleep, I got out of bed and walked over to my desk. I sat at it and picked up the family-sized bag of peanut M&Ms I'd gotten for Micah. There's a commercial that asks what you would do for whatever ice cream they were advertising. Well, for Micah it was, what would you do for peanut M&Ms. Seriously, he had been addicted to them. I'd planned on giving the bag to him when he recovered. I'd toss one in the air, and he'd catch it in his mouth. That's what we always did until he almost choked one day. Two minutes later, he was laughing and eating them like nothing had ever happened.

I picked up my phone and swiped through the photos. Cute ones of when Micah went out to eat with my family. He and my dad standing together. Micah smiling and posing while my dad had a crooked grin and looked as stressed as usual. Many of our memories were from school. Football games, dances, hanging out after class. I tried not to cry, but the thought of being at Lincoln High without Micah seemed too much to bear.

The days and nights between the funeral and the day I went back to school blurred together. My parents said it was time to get back to the world of the living. What? Had I been a vampire or something—vacationing in the world of the dead? Okay, Micah had been right. My jokes weren't funny.

I felt numb walking into Lincoln High. Everything seemed blah, like a movie that had gone from color to black and white. Or maybe food with no flavor. Yeah, that was a better analogy. I expected everyone to be weird. We were all mourning. Micah's best friend met me with a hug. A hug that meant everything. It said, *I understand your never-ending pain.*

We were equally surprised to see each other back at school so soon. I could tell he'd been crying. Just being there, in our hall, without Micah felt off. It was going to take a while to get used to.

"Come on, Chase. Stop it," I said, wiping away a tear that rolled down his cheek and over the peach fuzz he called a mustache. He and Micah had always joked they'd be shaving soon. "I know," I said. "Being here without him is hard."

Chase sniffed and ran his hand over his short dreadlocks. "He was like the heartbeat of this place, wasn't he? Maybe it was too soon to come back."

"I don't believe there's ever a right time." It was a fact. Even if we would have come back a year later, Micah still wouldn't have been here, and being at school would have felt just as awkward.

Chase opened his jacket, revealing a button pinned on the inside with Micah's yearbook photo.

I touched it gently. "Gone, but never forgotten? Whose idea was that?"

"I don't know, but the whole school got them."

"That's so very 80s of them."

"Don't worry, I grabbed you one." Chase leaned against the locker behind him. "Did you see the display case on the way in?"

"The memorial of all the students we lost to the virus? Yes. I didn't know there were twelve."

"I don't think I can take it happening again. Even if I don't know them. Maybe I should see if my parents can have me transferred to a new school."

I opened my locker and lifted my books from the shelf. "And leave me here?"

"You can come with," he said with a grin.

"I was about to say," I quipped.

Chase cleared his throat. "I know this all just happened, but I cannot get used to not seeing Micah running up the hall, late for class." He held his hand toward the side entrance. "I mean, like right now, he should be coming through those doors." Chase shook his head. "He always ran late, didn't he? And when I picked him up, he made us both late."

"Yeah," I said, trying not to picture it. Micah had always been late because it had been his job to get his younger siblings off to school. His mother worked crazy hours. At that time in the morning, she would have either already left for work or just gone to sleep after a night shift. And he never complained about it—not once.

A few other students joined us, all wearing Micah's button. Most expressed similar sentiments. Everyone missed Micah and expected things to be different. I listened and offered support.

That was just how I was. No matter how much I was screaming inside, I kept my feelings hidden behind that door, while I did my best to encourage others.

Chase walked me to class and continued on to his own, a head taller than everyone else in the hall—even with his shoulders slumped and hands in his pockets.

As I entered, a boy rushed up and knocked into me as he went inside. I stumbled and almost dropped my books. He glanced over his shoulder. "Oh, sorry, Brie."

I ignored him and looked around for a place to sit. *I can do this. Take it day by day,* I told myself. Shannon's twenty-braceleted arm shot up when she saw me. She patted the chair beside her, and I went and plopped down into it.

"Thanks for saving me a seat," I said.

She pulled her braids out of the back of her jacket. "Of course. I've been doing it every day until the bell rings. I'm glad you're back. None of these heifers will let me copy their work," she joked. "So how are you? Are you okay?"

"I'm managing," I replied as I took out a notebook and a pen.

"Me too. He was a good guy. I'm going to miss him."

It was kind of Shannon, but at the same time I thought, *OMG! How many friggin' times am I going to have to hear "are you okay" today?* The words were my new pet peeve. I decided the next person who asked me was getting shot in the face with a rubber band.

"Here." Shannon passed me a slip of paper.

"What is this?" At a quick glance, it looked like Monopoly money.

"A gift certificate from me. People don't know what to say when someone dies. Some can be downright rude. That certificate entitles you to five slaps. Whoever you point at, I'll commence to slapping."

Usually, I would've howled with laughter at her antics. There was no doubt in my mind Shannon would do it. Instead, I smiled and acted like I was paying attention to the teacher.

For the next few days, I sat through my classes, listening to the hum. That's what I called the voices of my teachers and classmates. I didn't understand anything they said. I heard hum of their tones intermingling, while I thought about other things. I think my teachers could tell I was somewhere else, but they didn't say anything or call on me to answer questions. One even caught me staring out the window and only smiled. A smile that said, *It's okay, you get a pass today.*

Each day at lunch, I forced myself to drink something. Eating was still out of the question. But that wasn't the hardest part of lunch period. The hardest part was leaving. So many memories took place outside of those double doors.

Micah's locker was at the end of the hall. Sometimes he shared mine, or I used his. I passed by the wall of windows that allowed you to see inside the cafeteria, hoping no one watched me having a flashback meltdown. *Don't do it, Gabriella. Don't you let them see you break.*

I choked back the tears, picked up my pace, and took a big breath, remembering an afternoon in that hallway when Micah had grazed my arm with his. I'd looked up at him. And when his eyes met mine, I'd felt something that I can only describe as divine. Peace and love, comfort and assurance. Micah had taken my hand and stopped me in my tracks. I remembered how he grinned—not a full grin, but just enough. His grasp was always gentle, and his hand warm and strong. His touch made me feel secure and safe. He had to have known I loved him. *Why didn't I tell him?*

I gave myself a moment to breathe deeply and collect myself before continuing to class. My head drooped as I walked, and I barely noticed the hum of students around me.

Before long, the last bell rang, and I was released from the prison of trying to act *normal*. But only for a few minutes, before I'd need to do another *normal* performance for my parents to keep them from worrying about my mental state.

I walked outside past a group of students who stopped talking when they saw me and into the throng of kids waiting at the crosswalk. The crossing guard blew his whistle, and we plodded across the street to the grocery store parking lot.

The school lot was so crowded that it was easier for my mother to pick me up over there. She smiled and waved as I approached her blue Tuscon. Then, acting as if the windshield were tinted dark enough for no one to notice, my mother leaned on the steering wheel, tilted her head, tucked her lips, and looked up her nostrils in the rear-view mirror. I normally would have tried to restrain my amusement; my mother was never embarrassed about doing those sorts of things in public, even pulling her pants out of her crack. Embarrassment was not a part of her DNA. Or was it discretion that wasn't? But as far as I was concerned, humor didn't exist anymore.

I opened the front passenger door, slid into the seat, and turned the air vent away from my face. My mother greeted me with her usual, "Hey, Brie-Brie. How was your day?" and some other stuff I barely heard.

"It was fine."

"Just fine?"

"Yep." I chewed on my bottom lip and shifted my backpack on the floor between my feet. A flash reflected in the side mirror. I almost gasped when I turned to it. Micah's dark brown eyes watched me. He looked exactly as he had that last time I'd seen him healthy, with his hair freshly cut and his face smooth. But there was something different about him now. He stared at me intensely before he faded into a reflection of the parking lot behind us: a shopping cart rolling by and a row of cars with kids climbing in.

"Brie, are you okay?" asked my mother.

I groaned internally. But no, I did not shoot my mother in the face with a rubber band. At that moment, I didn't even remember I'd said I would do that.

"Yes, I-I..." I couldn't find words, so I just stopped talking, stumped. *I'm losing it.*

We drove in silence, and my mother glanced at me every couple of minutes. My hand rested on the center console between us. At times, my mother grabbed my hand and gave it a light reassuring squeeze. Other times, she rubbed it.

When we got home, she dropped me off in front of the house. I hurried inside, up the stairs, and straight to my room. I threw my backpack and jacket on the bed, then paced the floor, clenching and unclenching my fists.

I stood in front of the mural behind my bed for a moment, staring at Micah's unfinished artwork. A portion of the wall was purple—my favorite color—and an array of flowers angled down from the ceiling and across the wall. The rest of the wall was white with only an outline of flowers.

I turned and faced the bathroom.

Okay. I shook my hands as if I were shaking water off and walked inside. I stood in the dark, staring at the mirror. *What are you waiting for?* I inched my hand toward the light switch. When I flicked it on, I wanted Micah to be there. At the same time, I didn't.

Just as I was about to flip the light on, my phone chimed and played "Always Be My Baby."

I gasped. It was the ringtone I used for Micah's calls only.

"Is that you?" I said aloud. "Micah?"

I shook my head and almost laughed. I didn't believe in that stuff. I pulled out my phone, almost expecting the text to be from him.

It was.

Gabby, I am not where I'm supposed to be.

I couldn't believe it. Right there on my phone—Micah!

1

---

1. Excerpt from *Never Really Gone* copyright © 2022 by L. B. Anne, JOA Press LLC, Florida.

ABOUT AUTHOR

L. B. Anne is best known for her Christian middle grade, Sheena Meyer, series about a girl with a special gift and a destiny that can save the world. L. B. Anne lives on the Gulf Coast of Florida with her husband and is a full-time author, coach, and mental health advocate. When she's not inventing new obstacles for her diverse characters to overcome, you can find her reading, playing bass guitar, running on the beach, or downing a mocha iced coffee at a local cafe while dreaming of being your favorite author. Visit L. B. at www.lbanne.com

Instagram: Instagram.com/authorlbanne
Facebook: Facebook.com/authorlbanne
Twitter: twitter.com/authorlbanne
Pinterest: pinterest.com/AuthorLBAnne

www.ingramcontent.com/pod-product-compliance
Lightning Source LLC
Chambersburg PA
CBHW022123310726
48972CB00007B/2173